The Blue Scarf

Celebrating
30 Years of Publishing
in India

Advance Praise for *The Blue Scarf*

'A brilliant set of stories that carries within it the very pulse of small town India – the taste and texture of its dreams and aspirations, hopes and betrayals, its struggles and resilience.'

– Namita Gokhale, writer and festival director

'I like Anu's stories ... more so because we both come from the same lingual and cultural roots.'

– Pankaj Tripathi, actor

'Anu Singh Choudhary's short stories find a home in that breach that creeps in between lovers, and dwelling here, quietly, painstakingly, they turn this breach into a hall of mirrors, whose curves reflect all of love's eccentricities: its dreams and dead ends, its fantasies and fears, how it makes of us odd little creatures unrecognizable even to ourselves. Kamayani Sharma's English translation is forthright and no-nonsense, which helps the sometimes brutal straight-talking of these modern urban love stories.'

– Akhil Katyal, poet, writer, activist and translator

'Stories of unfulfilled women, determinedly looking for fulfilment, unconventional, uninhibited, unafraid if uncertain – that's the world Anu Singh Choudhary writes about authentically and feelingly. Her prose is light and playful or ruminating and flowing, depending upon the angle she adopts to look at her urban subjects. The women in the stories of *The Blue Scarf and Other Stories* are searching keenly, relentlessly. As a reader, I felt the restless anguish of their search, as a writer I admired the honesty of the writing. The translation of Choudhary's contemporary Hindi by Kamayani Sharma is smooth and effortless.'

– Anukrti Upadhyay, author

'Writing is a very lonely, gut-wrenching job. Very few authors manage to carve out believable characters while living with their anxiety and fears in parallel. Anu however excels at it. I am always left surprised by her ability to dig deep within herself and create something so beautiful yet simple. We've had parallel journeys in many a way and like all journeys that start from a small town our struggles are to keep our roots intact and yet be contemporary. Anu has always pushed the boundaries of her craft and with each passing piece of work, I have seen her grow stronger and fearless, and yes, contemporary.'

– Suresh Triveni, film director

'I have been privileged to work with the "screenwriter Anu" who brings great sensitivity, deep understanding and a keen sense of observation to the films she writes. She brings the same compassion for the characters in *The Blue Scarf* which, like a woman's closet, contains colourful, joyful, eclectic and enriching episodes of their lives. Through these stories, I was compelled to reflect on my own life, its turning points and it left me warm and beautiful. I am so happy to have found a companion in this book that I will now carry in my own life and in my own stories.'

– Arati Kadav, film director

'Anu Singh Choudhary writes with courage and recklessness yet retains tight control over the smallest moments. As a writer she surrenders to the story, trusting her characters to illuminate the way as they navigate conflicts in search of their own authentic truth. Anu's short stories are evocative and emotive, delicately weaving loss, grief and guilt into exquisite patterns that reveal the warp and weft of relationships. Sometimes the edges are raw and jagged, like life itself. Anu is both a student and a master of the moment. As the characters in the stories claim agency and selfhood for themselves, the reader feels infused with energy too. Anu's writing offers piercing insights, the gift of attention and a gentle landing.'

– Natasha Badhwar, writer

'Anu writes with deep empathy and insight. Her writing has that quality of witnessing the journeys of many, especially women. If you read them, which you must, you might make a rare discovery about yourself in her stories.'

– Smriti Kiran, creative producer, consultant and curator

'*The Blue Scarf* is Anu Singh Choudhary's writing as we know it over the years – insightful, delightful and intuitive. Her characters start with utmost disarming simplicity, like meeting a stranger on a train journey, but by the time you reach your destination you realize how truly layered and beautifully complex her world is. These stories will take you on a trip down emotional lane, and I can bet you will come out a shade different by the end of it. Don't miss it.'

– Sandeep Modi, film director and screenwriter

'Anu, in her writing, has the rare ability to enable the exact sense and mood of what she is looking to communicate. Reading her work is a slowdown experience, [it lets you] experience words like feelings, which stay with you for a long time after you have put the book away.'

– Sanyuktha Chawla Shaikh, screenwriter

The Blue Scarf

AND OTHER STORIES

ANU SINGH CHOUDHARY

Translated by

KAMAYANI SHARMA

HarperCollins *Publishers* India

First published in India by HarperCollins *Publishers* 2023
4th Floor, Tower A, Building No. 10, Phase II, DLF Cyber City,
Gurugram, Haryana – 122002
www.harpercollins.co.in

2 4 6 8 10 9 7 5 3 1

First published in Hindi as *Neela Scarf* by Vani Prakashan

P-ISBN: 978-93-5629-394-6
E-ISBN: 978-93-5629-395-3

Typeset in 11.5/16 Adobe Calson Pro at
Manipal Technologies Limited, Manipal

Printed and bound at
Thomson Press (India) Ltd

For Adit & Adya, Advay, Vidit & Vidya.
And for every child who dreams of a fairer and kinder world.

Contents

First Look

SUSHILA CHACHI WAS BESIDE HERSELF WITH apprehension. After all, it was one of those things – you can imagine the state of the heart when it gets what it desires! It was not easy to find a good boy for one's daughter. That too, one who lived in Delhi! It was sheer luck that we found this one. Sushila Chachi had begun fearing that like her, her daughter too would end up spending her whole life in the village, smearing cow dung in the courtyard. Making rotis as she blew on the firewood heating the earthen stove. Envying city-dwelling relatives who would descend during the summer holidays …

It hadn't come to that. Her quarrels with Vinod Chacha had borne fruit this one time. She called me.

'I'll come to your place. That's where the *dekhvaki* will take place, in Delhi. We won't be an inconvenience to you and *mehmanji*, will we?'

'No, Chachi. It's our good fortune to host you. It'll be a chance to get together for a few days. When are you planning to come?' I asked, glancing at the gap winking beneath the door curtain.

I was worried about how I'd accommodate a *dekhvaki* in my two-room home. Where we were from, this ritual of the groom's family meeting a prospective bride for the first time was very intricate. It was no less than a whole ceremony! If things worked out, well and good, otherwise the mourning period to process the disappointment of rejection could last two months. Who knew this better than I?

When my husband got home from work that evening, I told him about the phone call with some trepidation. Thank God he was in an upbeat mood. He became excited too. 'Let them come. Facilitating a girl's marriage is a way of earning good karma. It'll be our good fortune to be of service to them. If not our kin from the village, who else will we be of use to?'

In fact, Sushila Chachi wasn't actually my aunt. In our family house in the village, four generations shared a courtyard. To be absolutely clear, Sushila Chachi's grandfather-in-law and my great-grandfather were paternal first cousins. They'd divided the family property between themselves many years ago, but the generations since hadn't yet done so. My grandfather was one of four brothers, all of whom had retained ownership of their ancestral land despite settling in the city. The cousin across the courtyard was an only son, with an only son of his own, Vinod Chacha. Everyone on our side of the courtyard had migrated to neighbouring cities one by one, leaving Vinod Chacha to look after the land, the cattle and the family home.

We kept going to the village during our summer holidays. The two households had separate stoves but shared the courtyard and main door. This is why, despite being separate units, we functioned more as family.

I had a very deep bond with Sushila Chachi. When the other children would spend their afternoons picking amaltas flowers and baby mangoes in orchards and gardens, I would sit in her room and listen to her singing. What a sweet voice she had! Embroidering saris, Sushila Chachi would sing folk songs about daughters being married off, and her magical crooning would have me sniffing and sobbing.

Put the palanquin
Under the neem tree,
O bearer of my paalki.
It's time to bid goodbye.

Mother says, visit us every day
Father says, only in six months
Brother says, come only for
Festivals and special occasions.
Sister-in-law doesn't want me to come at all.

Mother sheds a river of tears
Father's tears wet his turban
Brother's tears wet my dupatta
Sister-in-law rejoices silently.

Ever since, I was convinced that a girl's greatest enemy was, in fact, the sister-in-law. Thank God I didn't have a brother!

However, every year I would send a rakhi for Sushila Chachi's son, Rohit. Shweta had played in my lap. I used to braid her hair with red ribbons. All summer, I would apply kohl on her huge eyes. As the two children grew up, I taught them letters and numbers each summer. In exchange, Sushila Chachi gave me many gifts. She would make red chilli pickle flavoured with tamarind specially for me. She would secretly pack *barabar ka achar, aam ki khatti-meethi, channe ka sattu, teesi* and *pedas* of pure *khoya* in a bag and deposit it in our room the night before we were to leave for Patna. The only problem was that I couldn't brag about her endless love to anyone in the family. Neither I nor she had any remedy for the jealousies of the other grandmothers, aunts and sisters.

We still didn't have a remedy. Three of my uncles lived in Delhi and I had many cousins scattered in all corners of the city. Despite this, Sushila Chachi had decided to arrange for her beloved daughter's *dekhvaki* at my place.

Actually, all the children of my generation had come from our small towns to Delhi for our education. All of us came to the city with one dream – of becoming an IAS officer. After somehow managing to get by in the B- and C-grade colleges of Delhi University, we had realized our limitations. After college, I too had started working at a call centre as a marketing assistant.

After three years of non-stop effort, my father had somehow succeeded in arranging my marriage. The boy's family was from a neighbouring village and his family background was just like ours. Just like my father, my father-in-law-to-be was a government employee. Because of his government job, they had a two-room government-allotted flat in Kanpur, where the rest of the family lived. Once a year, they too would go to their ancestral village, for Holi or Chhat Puja. Just like my father, my father-in-law-to-be nursed a doomed-to-remain-unfulfilled ambition to move to his village after retirement. Even so, both he and my father had bought a couple thousand square feet of land and built homes in their respective cities.

Just like me, my husband was neither from a village, nor did he truly belong to his small town, and he hadn't succeeding in making Delhi his home either. We uprooted people can only pretend to have put down roots! One who can't put down roots in his native soil can't grow anywhere else.

My husband was an assistant sales manager in a private company. With four lakh rupees in cash, Papa couldn't have found a better son-in-law. Besides, I had two younger sisters. And so, after a total of three *dekhvakis* and rejections, when I was asked to go see him, I had gone without any expectations to Priya Complex in Vasant Vihar in Delhi. When he said he lived in Vasant Kunj, I understood that for him the border of Vasant Kunj extended to Kishangarh, in the same way that for me, living in Nilauthi Village was no less than living in Paschim Vihar's posh Meera Baug colony.

My wedding had taken place in the village. Sushila Chachi had taken over all the responsibilities of the mother of the bride. She had embroidered and stored saris and bedsheets for me. By the time Grandma awoke for the morning song at dawn, Sushila Chachi would wrap up chores in her kitchen and come to our side of the courtyard, busying herself with boiling milk and brewing tea. Come evening, when the women gathered to sing, Sushila Chachi would touch the first chord.

The peepal tree dances
Through the spring breeze
Father sleeps peacefully on his cot
Under the tree
Mother of the daughter, though
Doesn't know how to sleep

Wondering how
The father of an unmarried daughter
can even sleep so deep.

Shweta and I would sit and talk indoors.

'You heard that, Didi? How dare the father of the bride rest easy? You're educated, city-bred and beautiful. If your wedding was so full of hurdles, I wonder how mine will go!'

I would laugh and tease her, 'You sound just like Sushila Chachi, Shweta.'

'Yes, Didi, what to do? I listen to this all day. Ma's tape recording starts at daybreak, "I'll wed my daughter to a city-dwelling boy. Will she stay here and plaster dung cakes all her life?" What kind of stubbornness is this, Didi? Is it that easy? How will Babuji come up with four lakhs like Chachaji?'

'It'll all work out, Shweta. Destiny ensures we reach our destination. Didn't you hear what the mothers outside were singing?'

Go father,
Find your way
To the city of Ayodhya.
Lives there the great king Dashrath
Gently offer him paan and supaari
Leaves of the tulsi plant
As gifts of the dowry.

Dear father,
If you pray with folded hands
You may just get Ram
To be your son-in-law.

'These words sound good only in songs, Didi. Even Shri Ram had to break Shivji's bow to win Sita's hand.'

Having been born and raised in the village, Shweta would speak to me with practical wisdom.

So then, who had agreed to break a bow for Shweta? How would Vinod Chacha put together enough money for a dowry that would attract a Delhi-based groom?

I postponed my questions for Sushila Chachi's arrival. In any case, I was aware of how enamoured she was of the city. She had only two goals in life – getting Shweta married into a city-dwelling family and making sure Rohit got a job in the city. If the city in question was Delhi, all the better.

Whenever I would visit the village, Sushila Chachi would dig for information about the city. 'Dear, what's your house like? You probably don't have courtyards there, do you? Well rid of this business of smearing cow dung. Do you get cooking gas easily? You probably don't need a hand pump either. Just turn on the tap and out gushes water …'

It wasn't difficult to appreciate the allure of the city for Sushila Chachi. Since childhood, we'd come to the village in our colourful readymade clothes while Sushila Chachi would order clothes for Rohit and Shweta from Chainpur Bazaar. Later, even Shweta would remark: what else but cheap country clothing is to be expected here?

Our diction, lifestyle and attitude had become that of city-dwellers. Ma would often speak only in Hindi. Aunt Sushila was mesmerized by Ma's chiffon-like synthetic sari and Papa's dapper pant-shirt combination.

'Brother, what a smart shirt you're wearing. Like an important officer. Their uncle spends the whole day wrapped in his dhoti, feeding the cattle and driving his tractor. I think he even smells like chaff.' I would giggle at Sushila Chachi's words. Often, in my nonsensical daydreams, I would imagine her dozing off on a heap of chaff.

I don't know if Sushila Chachi stopped associating Vinod Chacha's body odour with chaff, but her love for the city had finally drawn her to Delhi.

Along with Shweta and Sushila Chachi, the whole of Pakvaliya village had descended upon the railway station! Pakvaliya was Sushila Chachi's native village and was known for its coarseness. Who knew how, despite being a daughter of Pakvaliya, Sushila Chachi's speech and behaviour was so full of sweetness!

I was utterly taken aback on seeing this wedding procession. How would I accommodate all these people in my two-rooms-with-single-toilet home?

Shweta leaped forward to hug me. I asked her, 'Have all these people come with you? Is the plan to abduct the groom? Is that what you're going for?'

'Oh no, dear. This suit was arranged by my big brother. So he had to come. Then there's my nephew, my sister, Sumitra Phua's middle son and there in that corner …' Sushila Chachi kept the introductions flowing without taking a breath.

'That's all very well, Chachi. But where will they all stay?'

'Why? Isn't there enough space in your house?' Her question stung.

Shweta's maternal uncle stepped in. 'Don't worry, dear. This isn't my first time in Delhi, is it? A brother-in-law of mine lives nearby, I'll go to his place.'

This was Delhi's specialty. Every adult member of every Bihari family had some relative or the other living here.

With Shweta and Sushila Chachi, I moved towards the bus stop. Vinod Chacha hadn't accompanied them.

'How could he have come in the middle of the harvest season?' Chachi explained sadly.

The three of us boarded bus number 604 from New Delhi railway station to Vasant Kunj. Chachi sat by the window and delighted with childlike glee in seeing the city flashing past under the springtime sun. It was as though she'd been granted a boon. Shweta remained quiet, stressed out by the crowd stuffed inside the bus.

We got off at Block D-3, Vasant Kunj. Each of us carried some luggage and, leaving Kishangarh's dusty bylanes behind, came to a halt at the first floor of a three-storey building.

Shweta plopped down on the settee in the living room. Sushila Chachi walked around, assessing my two-room home.

'You must have to stand and cook, babooni? That's good. All these years sitting and cooking on the earthen stove has given me knee pain. This is a small home, easy to clean. Sweeping a huge courtyard will only lead to backache.' Shweta said nothing, merely looked around.

It was Saturday, which meant a holiday for me. I had loaded the washing machine before leaving home. Shweta and I gathered the laundry to take it up to the terrace to dry.

On seeing the view of Kishangarh from the roof, Shweta was even more dismayed. 'Oh God! What a crowd, Didi. Houses are like matchboxes here!'

'This is nothing, Shweta. Wait till you see Gurgaon. Your head will spin when you see all the buildings touching the sky, really. By the way, how did Chachi find this Gurgaon boy?'

'My maternal uncle is childhood friends with the boy's father. They shifted to Delhi from Pakvaliya about twenty-five years ago. It was Mamaji who first spoke to the boy's family. Didi, the matter of my proposal photograph caused such a furore at home! Ma kept insisting that we'd get my photo taken only at one Prem Studio in Delhi. That's where yours got taken, isn't it?'

I laughed. I recalled not only the experience of having my photograph taken, but also how my mother went around saying to everyone in the village, 'Not that anybody would ever reject our Richa, but we made sure to get her photographed at Prem Studio. Sure, it was a couple of hundred rupees extra, but the boy's family liked it at once.' With great sleight of speech, Ma glossed over the part between the boy's family liking the photo and liking the girl and her dowry.

'So did you get that photo taken or not?' I asked Shweta, laughing as I returned to the present from my flashback. 'And the money, etc.? Has that been discussed?'

'Not yet, Didi. The boy's family is saying that we should give whatever we can afford, as a blessing. I am very anxious, Didi. Lest Ma's ambition to get me married in the city prove too costly.'

'What is your wish, Binni?' I asked, meeting Shweta's gaze.

'To be honest, I don't care whether it's village or city. I just want that my marriage doesn't become a cause of trouble for Ma and Papa.'

How do daughters all think alike! How do they all find reasons to compromise for the sake of marriage?

Shweta didn't need a Prem Studio photograph, after all. The boy's family liked her in the photo from Chainpur. The *dekhvaki* was fixed for the following Wednesday evening.

Everyone was to meet at a mall in Gurgaon. I took leave for half a day and my husband for the full day. We booked a taxi.

Sushila Chachi got busy organizing everything for the 'first look'. Sunday was spent finding a beauty salon and deciding on a sari. Chachi didn't want there to be any lapse at all.

On Monday morning, my husband left for work early and I followed suit at eleven o'clock. I gave Chachi and Shweta all the information they would need regarding the kitchen as well as important phone numbers. When we returned late in the evening, we recognized neither our home nor Chachi and Shweta!

Sushila Chachi had transformed not only our two rooms but, thanks to the trip to the salon, herself too. Seeing her in a salwar suit, sitting and smiling on an embroidered bedsheet in a freshly decorated room, both my husband and I thought that we'd walked into the wrong house. Shweta, with her hair trimmed, was standing in a corner and giggling.

I laughed and hugged Sushila Chachi. My husband smiled and said, 'The boy's family will accept the alliance even if we send you instead of Shweta, Sushila Chachi.'

She blushed as though someone had rubbed the pink of her *odhni* onto her cheeks.

Chachi was ecstatic. Dinner was ready. Shweta got busy laying the table as Chachi prepared hot rotis. As her wrists rolled the pin on the board, she began a song about Ram and Sita's wedding:

As Ramchandra gets ready
For his wedding
A bird flies away
With the wedding metal pot

Then, speaking to herself, she struck her forehead with a palm in exasperation, 'Oh God, what am I singing? Shouldn't be singing a song of misfortune.'

She continued:

Ramchandra is getting ready
For his wedding
Amidst great pomp and show
All the sages bless him
Such a handsome groom!
The dusky groom in yellow attire
We welcome him home
We welcome this handsome groom.

On the day of the dekhvaki, it was as though Sushila Chachi's feet had grown wings. Since eight in the morning, she had been to the corner shop thrice, at times for the sacred roli thread, at other times for the ceremonial *akshat* rice, then for the vermilion, once for jaggery. She had laid claim to the pooja corner at five in the morning. Goodness knows how many times she'd prayed.

'Richa babooni, once she's married, I'll go pray to Murar Baba by myself. I'll offer laddoos at the temple by the paakad tree, walk barefoot to Mehdar to pray to Baba Mahendranath. Just once our course is set.'

Poor Shweta sat and listened to her, nervous and withdrawn. This would be the most important exam she would ever take. If she cracked it, well and good, else she faced the prospect of having to retake it!

I draped Shweta in my sari, the yellow georgette enhancing her vivacity.

'No sister-in-law of mine can be rejected.' At my husband's words, Sushila Chachi beamed. Piling into the taxi, we set off towards Gurgaon.

The rest of Chachi's family met us there. Her jaw dropped on seeing the size of the mall. She had never seen this side of the city. Huge showrooms. Proclaimed to be 'on sale', colourful clothes, shoes and watches lured you from full-length display cases, all with the goal of ripping you off!

In the mall, our wedding procession resembled a band. Attired in colourful kurtas and starched dhotis, our male relatives stood out. A total of twelve people were present for Shweta's *dekhvaki*.

We put some tables together in the restaurant and sat down to wait for the boy's family. He soon arrived with his parents and seated himself at the other end of the table. His father started conversing with Mamaji while his mother came and sat beside me and Sushila Chachi.

It was my husband who, after the customary greetings and small talk, first addressed the boy. He worked for his father, in the business of operating taxis. After marrying, he planned to set up a factory producing shirts and T-shirts in Manesar near Gurgaon.

The conversation awkwardly wound towards the heart of the matter. After much effort, it was Shweta's Mamaji who brought it up, 'If you like the girl, let's proceed?'

The boy's father laughed and grabbed his hand, 'We like the girl, let's proceed. We know what you want to ask. We want nothing but your daughter. We are, after all, business folk. With this deal, we're interested only in maximizing profits for both parties.'

Mamaji stared at his friend's face. Whoever thought of the *girl's* family's profits while discussing her marriage?

'I'm sure you know that we have no kin in Pakvaliya. But we do have some land there. You know that Ram Khilawan, don't you?'

Mamaji shook his head.

'All we want is that you buy it. You'll get land and we'll get money. If we had to ask for money, we'd have done so upfront. But we're thinking of your profit too. We're friends, after all.'

Mamaji looked at Sushila Chachi. She had not expected such a deal at all! Had they asked for money or assets, the matter might have been up for negotiation. But how could they bargain over this offer? Chachi's heart, that had been bursting with glee at the prospect of an alliance with a family that owned thirty-seven acres of land, now shrank. I recalled my father's maxim – marriage should always be arranged between equals.

Without further discussion, the *dekhvaki* came to an end. As they exited, Mamaji put a hand on Sushila Chachi's shoulder and said, 'We can proceed with the suit if you wish, Sushila. But if you ask me, it's not a great match.'

Chachi said nothing, just got into the car.

The half hour it took us to get home felt like half a century. Shweta and Chachi were quiet; my husband and I weren't quite sure how to console them. I could almost hear the words echoing across the village courtyard and broadcast through phones in various cities like a BBC bulletin, 'This is what she gets for doing a *dekhvaki* in Delhi. Who told her to bound away to show her daughter off in the city?'

I was absolutely sure that this was what Sushila Chachi was also thinking.

The despondency hadn't lessened even by the time we got home. But once she had gulped down some tea, Chachi's mood changed like sunshine transforming a rainy day.

'So what, *mehmanji*? This sort of thing happens during a *dekhvaki*, isn't it, Richa *babooni*? It was a good excuse to spend a few days with you. Else when would we have had the good fortune? Isn't it, Binni? Aye Shweta, am I wrong?' At Sushila Chachi's words of bittersweet consolation, a depressed Shweta gave a small, nervous smile.

Using my phone, Chachi called Vinod Chacha. 'Oof! The boy was not at all suitable. He came wearing jean-pants. Wore his hair long, till his neck. On the one hand, there's Richa's husband and on the other hand, this boy acting like a big city man. Listen you, call up the priest from Kusumwari. Tell him we accept that suit. That boy's a high-school teacher, he's comfortable, what's the problem? Will our girl, used to huge courtyards, be happy in these tiny matchboxes of the city? Besides, it'll never come to us having to sell our fields to settle in the city. And listen you, tell the Kusumwari family that we'll go straight to the wedding, none of this *dekhvaki*-ukhvaki. You're listening, aren't you?'

The Last Puff of the Cigarette

EACH CORNER OF THE ROOM HAD BEEN SPRUCED UP. The light from the cane lampshade was just as she liked it – scattered on the one spot where inside a glass vase, bunches of narcissus were haphazardly thrown.

As the light fell on it, she quickly counted the colours spread on the tablecloth underneath the vase. One colour looked faded. Why hadn't she paid attention while buying it? Then again, she also hadn't thought that her useless dreams would be devoid of colour.

While changing, she noticed the bottle of lily of the valley. The last drops of a dying fragrance remained. Nothing is permanent. Even the intimacy of a fragrance that appears to belong to us will one day dissipate.

In the fridge were beer bottles from the last party whose fate had to be decided. At the party she'd told a colleague that there was no real difference between the smell of beer and that of horseshit. No sooner had she said this than everyone at the party abandoned the beer and clashed over the Breezers. Those Kingfisher bottles were still lying here. Orphaned.

'It's a good hair conditioner,' her roommate's words reminded her of the odour emanating from the army camp's stables in the valleys of Sonmarg.

'It'll be a mismatch. Your hair, this smell ... like Sonmarg and the army camps.' And so, plans for the remaining beer were once again postponed.

She didn't know what she was thinking when she placed two mugs of beer on the dining table. Chilled beer would harm her throat and she wouldn't find anyone to do a voiceover for her primetime show the next day.

Her roommate was going to return late tonight, after suffering a long evening of pointless debates over apple juice at a client's party. The Boy never stayed over for longer than an hour these days. Distance was a plausible excuse, but rather than the distance between Rohini and GK 1, it seemed to her that there was a distance between hearts. Sort of like the distance between Mars and Venus.

When we are determined to maintain distance, any excuse will do.

Anyway, the Boy would take at least an hour and a half to get here from Rohini. That meant she had a lot of time. Enough time to cook *rajma-chawal* for dinner, organize her wardrobe, preen herself on reading a book, oblige the newspaperman by reading an article from the weekly delivered *TIME* magazine. Or to decide what to do with her directionless relationship. This last was the easiest task, because it was no longer difficult to decide what to do with this relationship.

She was from a small town; she could go back. There was peace there, a buffer, and none of the rigmarole involved in getting to know someone. And it was an easy love, too. So-and-so's daughter would be Mr Such-and-such's daughter-in-law, no complaints. They were childhood friends. This wasn't an inter-caste marriage. The families knew each other, so she would be welcomed with a six-inch thick, padded red carpet. There was no conflict, an easy way. Lifelong ease.

The heart kept questioning. The heart kept answering.

Then why this stubbornness? What was this feverish desire that seemed incomplete even as it was being fulfilled?

The stubbornness was because life's ease is often its biggest challenge. The harder our struggles, the more easily we are satisfied with the illusion of living. And what of desires? It is their very nature to be feverish.

So what was to be preserved?

Who are we to preserve? Through our lives, the task of collecting the scattered is indeed ours.

And so? What was to be achieved finally?

The cigarette. The cigarette was to be had for now.

If not a habit, then a craving.

If not a craving, then a need.

She had called the Boy and instructed him to get Classic Milds. There was still an hour before the Boy got here.

Sixty minutes. Three thousand six hundred seconds.

Why should a need be kept waiting so long? She decided to go down and buy cigarettes by herself. As she glanced at the red toenails gleaming in the glittery red slippers, she was reminded of another of her roommate's triumphs. Why did she give in so quickly? Now she'd have to go home and do the added work of finding the nail-polish remover. If she spent twenty seconds on each toenail, she'd save 200 seconds. Finding the remover would take 600 seconds.

In GK, no eyebrows are raised upon seeing girls buy cigarettes, and alcohol is easily bought at the supermarket. Cigarettes were bought and so was a green apple-flavoured vodka. While making the purchases, she'd even netted 600 seconds in the bargain.

Bargains of time were not that difficult.

There was no Internet, else she could have made a nice cocktail. She called the Boy to ask whether vodka could be drunk neat. 'I'm at the last traffic signal' – this response contained nothing resembling an answer to her question. Neat it is, she mused as she poured vodka into a glass and took out a cigarette from the pack of Classic Milds, to light up.

'You'll never learn to smoke a cigarette, girl.' She remembered her roommate's taunt. She held the cigarette in her left hand and the lit matchstick in her right.

'Take it in your mouth and light it, then draw a puff.' She kept following her roommate's directions in her head and voila! A lit cigarette was in her hand. 240 seconds...

The phone rang. It was Ma. 1200 seconds, at the very least. She was to marry and reproduce on time. People tend to gossip ... 200 seconds ... the marriages of Chinki-Pinki-Bittu-Gudiya from the neighbourhood had been fixed. A description of the prospective grooms' families and dowry arrangements ... 600 seconds ... attacks on her waywardness and deviance ... 600 seconds ... a bonus!

The doorbell rang and she was relieved of the phone till morning.

'I couldn't get the cigarettes. Couldn't stop the car anywhere,' the Boy said.

'I got them, want one?' she asked.

'Oh! No thanks,' the Boy replied.

'Vodka or beer?' she asked.

'Is this a special occasion?' the Boy asked.

'It's my second anniversary on the job. I've promised to remain there for the next twenty-five years,' she said.

'What do you want?' the Boy asked.

'Ask me what I don't want. That'd be easier to answer,' she said.

'Do you have a disease that makes you disagreeable?' the Boy asked.

'And you discovered this today, after all these years?' she said.

The Boy attempted unsuccessfully to change the evening's soured mood. He asked, 'Want to eat? Let's go out?'

'Black salt goes well with green apple vodka,' she answered.

'I give up,' the Boy said.

'I've known you were a loser since we were kids,' she replied.

'What's wrong with you? I feel like shaking you up,' the Boy responded agitatedly.

'You won't because I don't permit it. You ask me for my consent before so much as touching me,' she remarked coolly, drawing a deep puff of the cigarette.

'Are you drunk?' the Boy inquired sweetly.

'What does it look like?' she quipped with equal dryness.

'Looks like there's no point. We're trying for nothing. I should go back home.' The Boy accepted defeat.

'The door's behind you. Get me another pack of cigarettes on your way out. My roommate might want one. We're not going hunting for it at midnight.' The girl ended the conversation.

'This is what happens when small-town girls come to Delhi to study. They become spoilt. At least retain some of your values. Is this what you came here for?' The Boy gave it his last shot.

'If this was your final salvo, it's wasted. Don't bother trying again.' The girl started pouring vodka into the glass, deliberately from a height so that the vodka's glug rang afar. At least as far as the Boy.

'I give up,' the Boy said.

'Take this vodka. You may need it. Buy an extra cigarette too. I forgive all your sins. Looks like our values came bundled in only my luggage when I came to Delhi. Take them with you. Return them to my home. Might as well discharge some duty of being a boyfriend … sorry … ex-boyfriend!' The girl took hold of the door.

The Boy gave her a sad look and spoke, 'Why do I feel like this is the last time I'm seeing you?'

'Better get a good look then. I won't ever look this beautiful again.' The girl kept holding the door and allowed her voice to drift.

The Boy gave her a lingering look, then left after imprinting his gaze on her face. A while later, the watchman delivered five packs of Classic Milds.

She finished smoking a pack as she waited for her roommate. She opened the second one only after the roommate returned.

'My efforts bore fruit. He won't be back.' She washed down the sudden hitch in her throat with a gulp of water.

'But why did you do that after all?'

'He should be at home, with his parents. He owes them his life. He didn't owe me anything. In any case, staying with me means a lifetime of tears.' She rested her head on her roommate's shoulder and spoke in a tired voice, 'I've known him since childhood. He won't change. And you see how I'm changing every minute, so rapidly. If he can't put up with me, he'll berate me. Cry. Scream. I accept his going away, not becoming fed up and leaving me.' She kept speaking monotonously, as though succumbing to the slow intoxication of the cigarette.

'You could have gone with him. He wasn't going to some unknown city,' her roommate noted for some reason.

'A city isn't unknown or familiar. We make it ours or don't,' the girl said, getting up from her roommate's side to leave.

'Didn't you love him?' was the roommate's last question. Sitting on the floor, looking into the eyes of the girl now standing next to her, she posed this tough question.

'I did. I do. That's why I didn't go with him.' Saying this, the girl took the cigarette from her roommate's hand to take a final deep puff and went into the bathroom to wash her hair with beer.

The Way Things Were

SUSHRUTA HADN'T TURNED IN HER HOMEWORK TODAY either.

Finding excuses to mock the teacher during class, insulting the other girls, giving absurd answers when called on – all this was second nature to her. Goodness knows how many times I had written a note to her parents in her school diary. But there had been no response from them. What sort of parent gives such free rein to their child?

'Sushruta Pandey, Sushruta … I am talking to you.'

'Yes, Teacher,' Sushruta said absently, not bothering to even stand up.

'You haven't done your homework today either?' I forcefully injected gentleness into my tone; my own voice sounded artificial to me. 'May I ask why?' Now my voice sounded dry.

'I've run out of excuses, Teacher. I don't have a new one.' This insolent response astonished me, as the other girls burst into laughter.

I said nothing. No, I wouldn't write a complaint in her diary today. I wouldn't tell the principal either. Nor would I discuss this in the staff room. It was all futile. The diary didn't reach the parents. Principal Ma'am would merely say, in her sweet lilt, 'You have to handle it, Suchitra. You are the teacher. You have to handle it very carefully.'

In five years of this job, I hadn't figured out the meaning of the 'very' that Principal Ma'am laid such emphasis on.

Ending the class, I made my way to the staff room. Even here, Sushruta's gaze followed me. How someone's eyes can make fun of you behind your back was something I'd understood only after becoming a schoolteacher.

I'd asked Sushruta to meet me near the library during the lunch break. Waiting for her at the window outside the library, I listened to the noise outside. From where I sat, I could see the school lawn and in it, girls bounding about, sitting in small groups, laughing, playing and chatting. They would grow up before my eyes.

The year I joined this school, Sushruta was in the third standard. Now she was in the eighth. I started this job when Siya was a year old. At Dheeraj's insistence I got an MSc. Then a BEd. I enrolled myself for a PhD. It was at his insistence that I agreed to teach at this school. 'I'll be away for six months at a time. In my absence, how will you fill the days, Suchitra? You need to go out, meet people and live your life. Don't bind yourself to Siya and consider yourself fulfilled.'

Dheeraj was right. But teaching growing schoolgirls is no joke. Especially if you're foolishly sensitive, have been disciplined about your own studies, and expect the same from others.

Returning home to a house without Dheeraj every evening and managing the responsibility of raising Siya alone had complicated my life manifold. I had the option of staying with my husband's family or mine. But after an age, you don't appreciate any sort of interference. You want to live on your own terms. In your own way. Despite the many challenges and many emotions that accompany loneliness.

'Teacher, will you lecture me here or in front of everyone in the staff room?' Sushruta's sarcasm interrupted my daydream.

'I haven't called you to lecture, Sushruta. Have you had lunch?'

'Yes, I had an eggroll in the canteen.' For some reason, Sushruta's voice had softened.

'I called you because I needed some help. You live in Gandhinagar, right? In A Block?'

'Yes, should I give you my house number? Will you come home to complain?' Sushruta was back to her acidic comments.

'Oho Sushruta, you're impossible! I said I needed your help. By the way, do you know the meaning of your name?'

'Yes, I do. I also know that my behaviour is the opposite of this meaning.'

'It's the same with me. My name's Suchitra but I'm not photogenic from any angle.' I had never brought up anything like this about my mountain of a nose and ordinary features in school, while at work. I wondered why I did so now, in front of this girl who never let up any opportunity to make fun of me.

'The thing is, Sushruta, we just shifted from Lalpur to Gandhinagar two days ago. I saw you this morning, standing at the bus stop, and realized we're neighbours. I don't know this area very well, nor any locals. May I ask your mother for some important information and phone numbers?'

Why was I telling this girl all this? No, this wasn't why I'd asked to meet her. I had something else to say! I could've thought of some other excuse to meet her mother. Sushruta too was regarding me with disbelief, scanning my face for lines that would betray my deceit. I was waiting for her to lose her temper: 'If you want to meet my mother, you could just say so. Why lie, Teacher?' But Sushruta didn't say anything, just kept looking at me.

'Do you have a pen and paper?'

I was shocked by Sushruta's unexpected response. 'Write your house number down, Teacher. I'll help all I can.' I wrote down my house number and gave it to Sushruta. For some reason, I was sure she'd come by after school.

After school, I went on my Scooty to pick Siya up from the creche. Once her nursery hours were over, the creche's staff picked her up from the bus stop and I took her home on my way back from school. Raising a kid as a working mother wasn't easy, especially if your husband spent six months on land and the remaining six sailing the high seas. That was why I believed in discipline and punctuality. The hands of the clock kept me busy. I had a goal fixed for every hour and every minute of my time. It might seem eccentric, but this quirk had kept me from full-blown insanity.

Hearing the bell ring in the evening, I instinctively knew it was Sushruta. Looking down from the balcony, I could see that she had come with a boy, on a motorcycle. I invited them both up. The drawing room was a mess. On one window hung a vermilion handloom curtain. The other was bare. I tried to make room by shoving the cartons on the sofas scattered in the room. Siya played on the carpet, pretending that the books were train compartments. The engine was an Oxford dictionary. I tidied the room as best I could in thirty seconds.

'Don't worry, Teacher, we won't stay long. Here, I have some numbers for you. I've told the maid, she'll come by at six.' She handed me a piece of paper. The handwriting on it was very different from the careless scrawls in Sushruta's notebooks. Each letter had been carefully inscribed. It contained numbers of the neighbourhood grocery store, milkman, plumber, electrician, handyman and carpenter.

'I didn't know you had a little girl. I'll get you the numbers of the doctor and hospital at school.'

I was astonished. This was the same Sushruta whose recklessness in class had driven me to the point of resignation! The same one because of whom I cursed my job at least ten times a day! This was the same Sushruta who had made me question my capabilities as a teacher at least eighty times in the past eight months!

'Who looks after your daughter when you're at work, Teacher?' I was not anticipating this question from a thirteen-year-old girl.

'She stays at the creche after her schooltime.' Perhaps a defensive tone had seeped into my voice. I promptly explained, 'When Siya's dad is home, he stays with her all day. When he's off to sea, I have to put her in the creche.'

But why was I defending myself to this girl? Who was she to ask me these questions? I wrung out the honey from my voice and once again assumed the mantle of the strict teacher.

'Some water? Your brother's been standing for a long time too. Why don't you both sit?'

Sushruta laughed. 'He's not my brother, Teacher. He's my boyfriend.'

Sushruta recognized the consternation and shock in my eyes and her lips relapsed into the mocking smile – a smirk. Ignoring the smirk, I asked her to sit. At the moment, I was unable to think of anything except making them some sherbet as a token of gratitude.

I went inside to make sherbet. Sushruta and her 'boyfriend' sat on the floor and played with Siya. I could see one advantage of sending Siya to a creche: she didn't take time to warm up to strangers. In the time it took me to serve Tang, the boy had assembled the books into a building for Siya and the three of them were chanting 'Qutab Minar-Qutab Minar' as they clapped and laughed.

Pasting an artificial smile on my face, I extended a couple of glasses of sherbet to the two. I thought to myself, what sort of mother didn't even know that her daughter was out loitering with her 'boyfriend'. Look at this girl's shamelessness, bringing him to meet her teacher.

After sitting for a while, Sushruta left. They both interacted more with Siya than with me. The boy didn't look ill-mannered or loafer-like from any angle. But I was unable to swallow the 'boyfriend' bit. Whatever was the meaning of 'girlfriend-boyfriend' for this generation?

I remained troubled for a long while. When Siya came to talk to me, I even told her off a couple of times. I couldn't put a finger on what was bothering me. Why was I thinking of Sushruta and Siya in the same breath?

Planning to wake up when Dheeraj called, I handed Siya a glass of milk and, blaming my frustration on my thyroid problem, retired early.

Sushruta was here again in the morning, with the maid. This time the boy wasn't with her. While I negotiated with the maid, Sushruta busied herself playing with Siya. Siya called her Shruti Didi. Sushruta probably asked her to call her that. Putting the maid to work, I asked both Siya and Sushruta if they'd like breakfast. They both shook their heads: 'no'. Sushruta asked permission to take Siya to the park. This time it was my turn to shake my head and say 'no', despite knowing that if Sushruta were to mind Siya even for a short while, I'd get a lot done. Curtains would be put up, the almirahs organized. Books arranged on the shelf. The milk and grocery might also get delivered.

But I was absolutely unwilling to let Sushruta become Siya's playmate. What if Siya were to become like her … no, no … it'd be best to keep Siya away from characterless girls like her. This time I said 'no' loud and clear. Sushruta left her landline and mobile phone number with me, 'Call if you need me, Teacher.'

I started thinking about Sushruta's mother again. Maybe she didn't have time for her daughter. Maybe problems at home were the reason she was like this. Otherwise, what sort of mother would be unaware that her daughter roamed free at all hours of day and night? And her father? It was possible that he had nothing to do with Sushruta. Or maybe, like Dheeraj, his job had him working away from the city. It was so difficult for a mother to raise a kid alone. For some reason, all thoughts pertaining to Sushruta had a roundabout way of coming back to my situation…

Every day, on my way to school, I saw Sushruta at the bus stop. How I wished I could take her with me on my Scooty. But my ego got in the way each time. I'd never had this sort of love–hate relationship with anyone. Not with any teacher, nor any student. Then why Sushruta? In class, I almost started avoiding her gaze. Maybe it was because I was afraid that befriending Sushruta would mean issuing an open invitation to drop by unannounced. Her closeness with Siya would discomfit me. And I didn't want any kind of conflict in my life.

But Sushruta was no less impertinent. One morning, she stopped me at the bus stop and climbed onto my Scooty without asking. Annoyed and angry, I took her to school with me. It became our daily routine. I might not have stopped my Scooty had there not been people around, looking at me. This was my rationalization, an unnecessary justification to myself. Maybe I was letting Sushruta in because it was convenient for me. She was my neighbour. I lived alone. Who knew when I might need her. In any case, I'd accepted the bit about the love–hate relationship.

But my slight unbending had the sort of effect on Sushruta that I hadn't hoped for in two years. She turned in her homework. She took the class tests and somehow scraped through. She paid the rent for riding pillion by working hard.

At the next parent-teacher meeting, I saw Sushruta's father for the first time in all these years. A middle-aged man, with a laptop case in his right hand and car keys in his left. From his clothes and mien, he looked more like a corporate type, more grandfather than father. 'Either time has aged us prematurely, or we've lived so long it shows,' my colleague Tahira had quipped in the staffroom that morning.

Walking ahead of Sushruta, he reached my desk. His soft footsteps lightened my mood and I smiled as I requested him to take a seat.

'You're Suchitra Ma'am, right? Sushruta's mother asked me to talk to you.'

I was very surprised. I had never met Sushruta's mother. He continued, 'I've also heard that you're our neighbour. This isn't the place, but please do come over to our house, not as Sushruta's teacher but as our neighbour.'

I smiled and nodded, repeatedly trying to redirect the conversation towards Sushruta's second-term results and her attitude. But her father wasn't willing to listen. The weather, the roads, the neighbourhood, the festival season – all these unimportant digressions made up the conversation. In all the years of my teaching career, never had I come across such a careless and negligent parent. Exhausted, I pushed the report card towards him and, after requesting him to sign the register, turned towards the rest of the waiting parents. At least they were interested in their daughters' studies. At least I wouldn't waste my time talking to them.

Christmas holidays had begun. Ranchi's weather was very pleasant this year. The sun settled down for a nice long stretch on the rooftop, from morning to evening. I'd suddenly started liking this Gandhinagar house a lot. There were wide roads in front of the houses. They were lined with gulmohar, amaltas, neem and cotton trees. Draw back the curtains from the window and winter sunlight flooded the room. Dheeraj was due to arrive in a few days. I was sitting on the balcony reading the newspaper. Siya was filling a mug with water from a bucket under the tap to water nearby plants. The doorbell rang. I peeped down. It was Sushruta with some lady.

In her attempt to open the gate, Sushruta had perhaps cut her finger on the latch. The lady draped in a black shawl rubbed her wounded finger zealously. I brought down the icetray from the fridge. Rubbing an ice cube on her finger, Sushruta came up with the lady. They had brought a box of chocolates for Siya. Despite my protests, the box was handed to Siya. For some time, they conversed only with her. As though they were here to see her, not me. I got up to make tea. Sushruta followed me to the kitchen.

'Why don't you sit with Mummy, Teacher. I'll make tea for both of you.'

Unwillingly, I plastered a forced smile on my face and returned to the drawing room. The lady in the black shawl smiled at me. Peeping out from behind her ears and going all the way to the parting on her head were bunched strands of silver hair. There was no attempt to dye them either. Paying close attention to her face, for some reason I was reminded of Waheeda Rehman. Just yesterday I'd seen her in a film – ah yes, *Delhi-6*.

This was Sushruta's mother? I had imagined an entirely different kind of woman. Why had I assumed that Sushruta's mom would be a Supermom type? A businesswoman who wore formal clothes, carried a laptop bag and spent all day at office. Could this autumnal, housewifely woman handle a feral creature like Sushruta?

'I have a request to make.'

'Yes, tell me.'

'Sushruta wants to learn maths and science from you over the holidays.'

'But I don't give tuitions.'

'Sushruta did say.'

What strange folk. No consideration for others' boundaries. Always ready to impose! That's why Sushruta was the way she was.

'May I take Siya downstairs? So you and Mummy can talk, Teacher.'

Now I was ready to explode with anger. First, they drop by without my consent, then they ask me to go against my principles, despite knowing that I didn't give tuitions. On top of that, this girl had the nerve to assert her claim to my daughter!

'Siya won't go anywhere right now.' As usual, I took my annoyance out on my daughter. Sushruta was looking at her mother.

'It's cold outside, dear. The sun's out but it's windy. Play with Siya here, Shruti. Teacher and I will sit out on the balcony, alright?'

Her voice has such a hypnotic quality that my anger automatically dissipated. Taking my cup of tea, I dragged a chair out onto the balcony.

'When does Sushruta want to start her lessons?' I'd voluntarily taken on the challenge that is Sushruta.

'Whenever you like. Please let us know when it's convenient for you. I want to tell you something else.'

'Yes, please do.'

'Sushruta is my younger child. She was born eighteen years into my marriage. I had a son, Shantanu. He hung himself one day. He was scared he'd fail maths and his dad wouldn't be able to take it. He feared his father would make his life hell. He found death easier. He thought it'd be easier for us to endure his death than his failing maths. I often think about where I failed as a mother. Wherever I recognized mistakes, I made sure not to repeat them with Sushruta. We've never asked her to study. Her studies aren't more important than her life.

Since her childhood, I've let her be. She's defiant but not out of control.' Sushruta's mother kept talking and I kept listening.

Consoling someone is the most difficult thing in the world.

This short chat had peeled back the psychological layers of Sushruta's behaviour. I now had no confusion or misgivings regarding her. It was true that I was unable to decide if I should tell her mother about the 'boyfriend' who roamed with her. I postponed the matter to the next meeting.

My heart was lighter now when I thought about Sushruta and Siya's friendship. I suddenly felt as though Sushruta would be my greatest achievement as a teacher. An achievement that I'd proudly speak of to many generations of students.

Sushruta started coming to my house every day. Solving algebra equations had eased ours as well. After tuition, I left Siya with Sushruta to attend to chores in the kitchen and home and run errands in the market.

It was the new year and Sushruta had once again brought her boyfriend to my house. 'Teacher, could you teach Dushyant too?'

Her audacity was shocking. I refused but Dushyant started dropping by uninvited anyway. He didn't do anything that would warrant my stopping him from coming over.

One day while explaining the law of gravitation, I started discussing the gravity of life with Sushruta. I finally asked her, 'Has Dushyant ever held your hand?'

Sushruta looked at me, startled.

'Have you two kissed?'

Sushruta didn't say anything, just kept staring at her books. I had got my answer.

'You are terribly young. I am sure your parents have explained to you that we are responsible for the mistakes we make in life. There are consequences. You do understand what I am saying, don't you?'

'Yes, Teacher.' Sushruta's attention was elsewhere now. She was thirteen years old. In seven years, Siya would be that age. Why did I keep seeing my own daughter in this girl? That day I sent Sushruta home early.

I shouldn't look for my daughter in Sushruta, nor should I try to mother her.

Dheeraj was here, so I give Sushruta a break for a few days. We next met in class. In the crowd of other schoolgirls. Dheeraj dropped me to school, so I no longer had any excuse to go with Sushruta. But it was true that I did feel her absence.

One day after school, Sushruta met me in the staffroom.

'I have something to tell you, Teacher.'

'Yes, Sushruta.'

'I've broken up with Dushyant. Over WhatsApp.' At this young age, they thought relationships were a game.

Who knew how badly they bruised their hearts and bodies? I was distressed once again.

'But we are still friends. Just not in a relationship any longer.'

I felt like shaking her and asking, 'At thirteen years of age, what relationship were you in, Sushruta?'

I'd started worrying about Siya again. Why was Sushruta like this? What could I do to ensure Siya didn't become like her? Sushruta's carelessness and indiscipline challenged me not just as a teacher but as a mother. She taunted my pride in Siya's strict upbringing and discipline.

With Dheeraj around, Sushruta barely came over. But I'd started receiving her homework notebook almost every day. She often came to the staffroom to ask me or Tahira for clarifications. We no longer discussed private matters. She didn't even ask after Siya, nor about when she might resume tuitions.

Sushruta did well in the final exam. Better than she'd hoped. But nobody came to pick up her report card, not even she herself. I kept it, planning to give it to her at her home. However, we left for Jamshedpur in the evening, to visit Siya's paternal grandparents. I returned to Ranchi a day before school reopened.

In two days Dheeraj was due back on his ship, which was why I didn't have time to even phone Sushruta. I asked Tahira, her new class teacher, about her. Sushruta hadn't come to school since it reopened. Once Dheeraj left, I took Siya and went to Sushruta's house for the first time.

I rang the bell for a long time before Sushruta's mother opened the door, coughing and panting. The tentative smile on her wan and sickly face made me think of a still pond disturbed by a thrown conker.

'Sushruta has gone to the market to shop for grocery.' She turned towards the kitchen, perhaps to fetch water for me. I implored her to sit and handed her Sushruta's report card. Without glancing at it, she continued talking in her wheezy voice, 'Sushruta said that your husband is in town, so you wouldn't be giving tuitions for some time. We couldn't come to pick up the report card. Sushruta's father would always go to pick up Shantanu's report, but …'

By now I had realized that in this house, the absent Shantanu was perennially omnipresent – in the walls, the showcase and the conversations. There were many photographs of him on the walls. In the one or two photographs of Sushruta, she was posing with Shantanu. It was not at all hard for me to gauge how his large trophies decorating the showcase dwarfed Sushruta's identity. I understood also why thirteen-year-old Sushruta sought a companion in her 'boyfriend' Dushyant.

An ailing mother stuck in a departed era, a self-absorbed father and a dead brother – how did Sushruta live with this all the time? How must she have felt when she brought her report card home and every conversation turned to her brother instead of her? How must every moment make her aware of her youth, even as she shouldered the responsibility to look after her parents and manage her home? How could she see a future in this household that was stagnating in the past?

Opening the door with her own key, Sushruta entered the drawing room, carrying a bag of vegetables. Her face lit up on seeing Siya. I got up, took the vegetable bag from her and set it on the floor, before handing her the report card.

'This is your progress report, Sushruta.'

I was unable to say anything else. I clasped her hand and added, in a thick voice, 'Tomorrow when you come for tuition, please teach Siya for an hour. She wants to learn from Shruti Didi.'

The Colour of Love Is Like Water

SHE TYPED THE NAME INTO THE GOOGLE SEARCH BAR again – Swati Prakash.

She had great faith in the power of the internet. Apart from delivering groceries and furniture to her house, the internet had helped her set up a successful business and find a husband.

Now that life had settled into a rhythm and there were no more battles to be won, it was on this very internet that she kept searching for that one name.

She had a strange relationship with this name. She was her best friend. Or was it her greatest enemy? Her biggest truth. Or was it a bit of youthful fantasy? She had never been able to understand the exact nature of her bond with Swati. Why does wax melt before a flame? Neither the wax knows, nor the flame.

But the internet has its limits. Some needs are all too human, and some solutions still subject to divine intervention. Even Google was incapable of connecting her to the one person she had spent years looking for. And if Swati Prakash had chosen anonymity, how could Shyamali find her? Still, for humans, hope blooms and wilts with the cycle of seasons, despite the endless and invisible despair of the worldwide web.

Might Swati have searched for her whereabouts with as much desperation? Would she have typed her name out with her fingers – Shyamali Sengupta? Could she have seen her on TV? How would Swati have felt seeing Shyamali on national TV commenting on the launch of a major IPO or the state of the Sensex following an election, or reporting on the corporate world's response to one of the PM's foreign visits?

Such baseless questions have no resolution.

Shyamali would never learn the answers anyway, because she couldn't find Swati.

Even if she were to find her, what would she say? Please forgive me? I had no intention of imposing my truth on you? In all these years, I have never managed to find a friend or sweetheart like you? Those we love the most frustrate us the most too? We flee from those we seek out?

It was possible that if Shyamali were to meet Swati, she wouldn't be able to express any of this. Or that Swati wouldn't want to hear any of it. It was also possible that even today Swati's eyes would be like a stranger's, which would kill Shyamali.

Even so, the desire to seek out and meet Swati was strong within Shyamali.

If every wish were to be fulfilled and Google search were to retrieve everything, who would turn to God for respite from the knots of misery and the pain of unrequited desires? That's why one day Romil – Shyamali's husband – took her from Delhi to Lord Balaji's door in Tirupati.

Amidst the material comforts of life, the one lack that ate away at Romil didn't really bother Shyamali. She didn't believe in the narrow-minded views according to which the only way a woman could be fulfilled was through her womb, with a baby in her arms. Shyamali was of the opinion that every person's self-fulfilment lay in collecting the many parts of their identity and assembling them like a difficult jigsaw puzzle. Still, in the quest for their own completion, husband and wife kept living a lie, denying the truth of many parts of their own identities.

Shyamali googled Swati Prakash because she was convinced that the friend she left behind forever twenty-one years ago was the only one who could help her find that one missing piece of the puzzle that she hadn't been able to find anywhere else.

Swati, not Balaji, was the solution.

And then, by revealing to Shyamali the sort of unbelievable miracle that she didn't believe in, Balaji won her lifelong trust.

Romil insisted that they wouldn't pay money or call on connections to obtain entry to the temple, even if they had to wait two days for darshan. Shyamali accepted Romil's decision without protest. At a government guest house in Tirupati, far from Delhi, deadlines and the stress of pitching the next project, she was enjoying the weekend.

Oddly, Romil too had plenty of time. Perhaps, apart from offering prayers, the idea was to embark on the process of baby-making!

On reaching Tirupati, in fact as soon as they left home, Shyamali had happily turned over all the decision-making to Romil. He was the one who finalized the guest house and decided the time for darshan – quarter to five in the morning. The evening before the darshan, Shyamali set off alone to wander in the by-lanes of the temple town.

There is no time of day more alluring than evening. Drowned in angst and love, infused with the colour of yearning, gliding in head held high under the weight of some enfeebling anticipation. No poet, no bard has yet been able to explain the link between evenings and the feelings of helplessness and restlessness that accompany them.

Coincidence – in the sense of serendipity or fate – why does it occur at dusk? No research has been done on this till now.

Was it coincidence or the miracle of a temple town that Shyamali found Swati there – standing on the threshold of a shop, holding a plastic bag, bargaining in Telugu!

They say that each of us has at least seven lookalikes somewhere in the world. Shyamali too assumed that this woman was a lookalike of Swati's, and didn't venture to address her. In any case, the waist size of the lady in front of her was at least five times that of the Swati whom Shyamali had seen twenty-one years ago.

But the way the lookalike's eyes paused and words stopped mid-flow on seeing Shyamali disclosed the familiarity between them.

'You can't be Shyamali,' It was a declaration, not a statement.

'Swati?' Shyamali's breath sped up as though she had just run six kilometres on a treadmill.

Swati said nothing, just moved forward and swept Shyamali into a hug. Shyamali hadn't imagined in her wildest dreams that the Swati, whom she had been searching for in the virtual world for years, would meet her like this.

Swati dragged Shyamali to her home. Ordinary alleys. An ordinary house. An ordinary south Indian husband. Two children. This was Swati's life now. Her present. All her joys and sorrows, her woes were gathered up in this pristine veil.

Swati was happy to see Shyamali. So happy that her chirpy, mixed Hindi-English-Telugu monologue and the coffee brewing in the kitchen were enough to embarrass her husband and kids. The three of them felt so awkward that they left Swati alone with Shyamali, exiting the house with some excuse or other.

'Are you happy … Swati?' Shyamali sipped the last of the filter coffee as she mustered the courage to ask.

Her eyes were on Swati. This rotund south Indian lady sitting in a colourless chair in a house inside a dense neighbouthood right behind the Tirupati market, basking in domestic contentment in her south cotton sari and mangalsutra, laden with gold jewellery – was not the Swati Shyamali knew. Had the colour and twinkle of her eyes and the ease with which she carried herself not been the same, Shyamali would never have accepted that it was Swati.

'Are *you* … happy?' Swati lobbed back the question in response.

As meaningless as these questions were, debating them was just as useless.

Shyamali was the college's Economics (Hons.) topper and a champion of the liberal arts. She was fluent in Tennyson and Tagore. When she sang Faiz in her earnest if untutored voice, those listening felt the blood quiver in their veins. Standing in the college auditorium, when she argued in favour of the Comprehensive Nuclear Test Ban Treaty, the opposing team would fall silent. She was president of the Students' Union. Shyamali had nowhere to go but upwards. She had come into this world to receive applause and collect trophies.

And Swati? Swati had come into the world as a shadow. First, she followed her elder sister throughout school. And then once she got into college on the basis of her marks, she became her roommate's shadow. Her ambitions were only that she score well in college, then at university, and then get a good job in a good office. That is all Swati expected of herself, and her family, who had migrated to Guntur from a southern Andhra village, was satisfied with this expectation.

By contrast, Shyamali had many admirers within and outside college. Girls wanted to be her, boys wanted to be with her. And Shyamali enjoyed the attention. The crowd surrounding her recognized Swati through her association with Shyamali.

Swati understood everything, but didn't care. At that age, the ordinary details of daily life are more precious, while the serious matters of life go unnoticed. The twinkle in a girl-friend's eye, the time spent with her, the moments stolen with her, are more important than worries about career. Besides, emotions like envy had never been part of Swati's character. This is why Swati and Shyamali never butted heads over any issue, in spite of the similarities and differences of their extremely typical Bengali and Telugu backgrounds. In the hostel, their friendship became an aspirational model. They weren't roommates, but fast becoming soulmates.

When the two went shopping at the mall and stood before the mirror in the trial room, they'd see themselves not as their own reflections but through each other's eyes. One day, Swati came out to show Shyamali the crisp blue sleeveless kurta she had tried on. Shyamali's heart galloped. That day, for the first time, she realized that what she felt for Swati exceeded friendship or camaraderie. She felt a kind of attraction, one that could not be properly expressed.

But understanding and expressing this emotion was fraught with danger. She had the wisdom to know that it was better to stay quiet. But in a weak, happy moment in the heady days of youth, Shyamali laid a new sort of claim to Swati.

It was Sunday. The delicate winter sunlight dripped from the windows and spread like honey over Shyamali's bed. In her quest for a sunlit corner, Swati got up from her bed and climbed onto Shyamali's. Leaning against the wall, as Swati attempted to bask her feet in the sun, her toe kept brushing against the half-reclining Shyamali's neck. Without warning, Shyamali sprang up with a jerk and pulled Swati into her arms. Shyamali recalled neither the reason for this sudden move, nor what had happened to her in the moment.

Shyamali didn't stop there. Along with her kiss, she placed onto Swati's lips a confession of her feelings. She wanted to hold Swati in a tight embrace, touch her as she had never touched anyone ever before. Waves crested in Shyamali's heart, an ocean of feelings for Swati. As quickly as they rose, the waves subsided and retreated into the river of reality.

Swati pushed Shyamali to the side.

She switched rooms the same day. Didn't even ask Shyamali what that kiss was about, or why it was so intimate. What was that moment in which Shyamali had become so weak? Were her leanings not, in fact, 'normal'?

Since that day, Swati became out of bounds for Shyamali. She neither cared to hear an explanation, nor did she tell anyone what had transpired. The kasturi scent of the bond between Swati and Shyamali, that had followed them around everywhere, was replaced by the stench of a friendship souring. Over time, even the other girls stopped gossiping about the issue. If they happened to come face to face in the mess, the library or the auditorium, Swati would look past Shyamali as though she were looking through a clear window.

Swati's unforgiving, indifferent gaze pricked at Shyamali like glass shards. The two didn't speak to each other through graduation. Shyamali couldn't explain herself, and Swati showed no intention of listening. This was the first and only experience Shyamali had of what the girls in hostel termed 'homosexuality' or 'lesbianism'.

After that, at every stage of life, Shyamali changed boyfriends like flavours of the month. While she studied in America, worked in London, lived in Mumbai, and settled down in Delhi – each time she got herself a new companion, a new body to discover from scratch. But she never found that sense of belonging she craved from her other half. Though Romil was the last station on her journey, she had stopped not for love but because, at thirty-eight, she'd felt compelled to.

'Did you marry?' Swati asked.

'It just happened. Romil is the one who brought me here,' Shyamali answered but indicated no interest in introducing her husband to Swati.

Nonetheless, Swati ended up saying, 'At least introduce him to me. I want to see what he looks like, this man who convinced you to tie the knot.'

Shyamali laughed. Many faces swam in her helter-skelter memories. She wanted to say that it was not a matter of the flesh, but a matter of the heart. When the strings of relationships bind neither hearts nor bodies, they cease to have any meaning. And the body is a strange thing. It can gleam with pleasure, like gold, under thc lightest touch of a stranger, while the brush of a beloved can render it as unfeeling as a lump of earth. But her words caught in her throat.

'The colour of love is like water, Shyamali. Whichever hue you infuse it with, it takes on that shade,' Swati told her.

In response, Shyamali kept looking at the gold glinting at Swati's neck, in her ears and on her wrists.

A gap of twenty-one years, and a great burden in the heart – Swati blew them away in a single breath. Nostalgia, or the longing for home, features those bylanes, streets, houses and people that are at the forefront of our minds. If left unattended, moments lost in the labyrinth of memories have no value.

Shyamali had been wandering without reason in the labyrinth of memories all these years. On the other hand, Swati accepted life entirely as it was in the present – of the current moment, of the now.

'The colour of your love is big, heavy gold, no?' Shyamali teased Swati, to which she quipped back, 'And yours is Swarovski.'

But for both, love was indeed water – one blue-green as it flowed through the sea, the other black like storm clouds pregnant with memories and pouring rain.

The chasm between their worlds was vast, so wide that despite Swati's sensitivity and Shyamali's wish to apologize, it was difficult to bridge. Romil and Swati's husband met, shook hands and said hello, completing the required formalities. The kids bade namaste to Shyamali Mausi, even making false promises to visit her in Delhi.

Then Swati did something that Shyamali neither expected nor wanted. As they were leaving, in front of everyone, she planted a lingering kiss on Shyamali's cheek – on her left cheek, right above the corner of her lips.

Swati's bus pulled out, and Shyamali was left behind in the throngs of hopeful devotees and darshan-takers – with Romil.

You're not supposed to propitiate Balaji with water, else today Shyamali would assuredly have mixed Swati's love in it, to see what the colour of this unnameable love came out to be. But that water poured down Shayamli's eyes and trickled into her long, lovely neck.

Shyamali would never again search for Swati Prakash.

The Lines of Destiny

'AY RANIYA ... RANIYAAAA! WILL YOU GET UP OR shall I kick you? Madam isn't out of sight for a minute before putting her feet up for a nap! This is the problem of servants with bad habits. They need constant supervision. Now will you get up or keep glaring at me?'

She who had been lovingly named 'Rani Kumari' by her mother had been turned into Raniya by Memsaab. This abbreviation of her name stuck to Rani such that not only Memsaab and her family, but her neighbours and Rani's own family had forgotten her real name. Child rights and child labour laws could go to hell, at the age of eleven Rani became 'Raniya' and Memsaab's magnificent bungalow became her world. It was coming up to three years working here, three years of being berated.

Every day Raniya would only wake up after kicks and curses, so why would it be any different today! The oppressive heat of May sedates even the most alert of people, and yet, according to Memsaab, Raniya was an old associate of Kumbhkaran. Unlike Raniya, her sleep did not come and go according to the whims and fancies of Memsaab.

Sleeping in random corners was an old habit of Raniya's. She could doze off anywhere and would often be engulfed by the weirdest dreams. Sweets and savouries, clothes and shoes, Binnu from next door, Muniya from the neighbourhood … they all gathered in her dreams. These days, Chhoti Memsaab was a frequent visitor. She just saw that Chhoti Memsaab…

'O Your Majesty! Are you going to just stand there and gawp at me or will any work get done?' Another taunt lobbed her way from the bedroom set her straight.

Raniya couldn't even dwell on why, in her dream, Chhoti Memsaab was sitting sadly and hemming an orange sari.

'Now if I start dreaming with eyes open, Memsaab will make mincemeat of me right here,' Raniya muttered under her breath. She didn't have time to even stretch her legs. Amidst the mistress's scolding, work had to be swiftly wrapped up.

But the storm was yet to hit bungalow C-147 in Sector 26. Memsaab's anger on seeing Raniya sleeping extended to the other servants as well. One by one, she reminded each one of their long-forgotten faults. Now they would come for Raniya! The cost of being the youngest.

As such, only Chhoti Memsaab's room was Raniya's refuge. Raniya quickly poured the fresh, cool water from the pitcher into the copper jug and advanced to Chhoti Memsaab's room. She could never understand why, despite having a fridge the size of a room and two more smaller fridges, Chhoti Memsaab chose to drink water from an earthen pitcher. And then there was Raniya's mother, who had been saving up for months for a second-hand fridge.

These days, she'd been given the responsibility of serving Chhoti Memsaab full time. The driver here, Ramesh Uncle, was Raniya's neighbour. The drivers, cleaners, electricians, cooks and domestic workers living in the Nithari slum had chosen to quickly consign to history the horrific memories of the Nithari child murders, as they returned to the rigours of their lives.

Raniya had still been learning to crawl when the murders occurred. Terrified, her parents had taken their family back to their village. But those who must risk their lives to make a living prefer the opportunities of the big city. At least here the risk is rewarded with greater remuneration. And so, the family returned to Nithari in six months. Raniya grew up listening to the stories of disappeared children in that very neighbourhood.

But dreading bungalows was not an option! On top of that, Raniya's mother was practical. She knew that if she left Raniya in Nithari, she would neither study nor work. Anyway, a couple of known leches in the big houses were better than a hundred strange ones. At least they were familiar devils!

And so, after much pleading with their neighbour Ramesh Uncle, Raniya's mother got her a position at the bungalow. She had been eleven then, she was fourteen now. Back then, her only jobs were massaging Memsaab's legs, fetching her water, ironing her clothes and arranging them in cupboards. Now she'd been promoted. Raniya had been appointed Memsaab's shadow. For the past few weeks, Memsaab had loaned her services to Chhoti Memsaab. Bequeathing their most trusty ayahs to daughters-in-law before bequeathing the keys to the safe seemed to be the tradition in these elite households, where disintegrated families lived with suspicion under the same roof and yet at a distance!

Raniya returned to her home in Nithari in the evening. Raniya's mother cleaned five homes while her father set up his vegetable cart on the Sector 37 road. Raniya was the second of three girls, and they had an elder brother. All of them worked. Ma's morning sickness suggested that the family wasn't done expanding.

Chhoti Memsaab's condition was the same as Ma's. The only difference was that after eight years of waiting, Chhoti Memsaab was going to become a mother for the first time. She had taken leave from work. The whole family was doting on her. Not that there were many family members living in the nine-room bungalow. There was Memsaab who had the whole house whipped into a frenzy all day, hot-tempered Bade Sahab and Chhote Sahab, always travelling for work, and there was Chhoti Memsaab. For these four people, a battery of seven servants stood at constant attention.

Raniya kept the water in Chhoti Memsaab's room. She was sleeping. Even the sound of the door opening didn't wake her. She spent all day in bed. As evening fell, she went to the terrace or balcony and sat there till the humid evening became the humid night. Here, Raniya kept delivering tea, dry fruit, melons, *shikanji, aam-panna* to her, one after the other. The last course included colourful pills along with the boiled vegetables and soup. By then it was time for Raniya to go home.

Raniya accompanied Chhoti Memsaab like a shadow. But who talks to their own shadow? Neither expects the other to speak. One keeps issuing orders with sad, silent eyes, the other follows them with silent alacrity. In their shared silence, they find an ease.

Which was why Raniya was shocked when Chhoti Memsaab broke the silence that day.

It happened just last Wednesday. Since Chhoti Memsaab couldn't bend, Memsaab had ordered Raniya to clean her feet, cut her nails and apply nail polish.

As Memsaab had instructed, Raniya brought a large tub filled with warm water. Without saying anything, Chhoti Memsaab soaked her feet in the tub. Raniya too said nothing as she regarded Chhoti Memsaab's fair ankles submerged in the warm water.

'What are you looking at, Raniya?' It was Bhabhiji who broke the silence.

'Your feet. They are so beautiful…' Raniya was unable to hide her admiration. She couldn't quite said that not just her feet, Chhoti Memsaab herself was so beautiful! Fair and lovely like Katrina Kaif. Ma often said that if a buffalo were to be given a coat of white, people would start worshipping it like a cow! And Chhoti Memsaab was indeed beautiful … she would be even if she weren't fair-skinned.

That day Raniya saw Chhoti Memsaab laugh for the first time, the hot May afternoon suddenly refreshed by rain. She laughed and said, 'These are all lines of destiny, Raniya. These feet have trod only soft ground.' Then after a beat, 'I've only been blessed with fields of flowers to walk on Raniya. Not the open skies that you can soar in.'

This statement of Chhoti Memsaab's left Raniya stunned for days. Even Chhoti Memsaab, who wore fine clothes and drove herself to office, considered her life unfulfilled. The grass does always seem greener on the other side. Chhoti Memsaab romanticized Raniya's life. Raniya envied Chhoti Memsaab's. Wouldn't it have been nice if on leaving the bungalow each evening, Raniya too could go somewhere else, driving her own car!

For the first time that day, Chhoti Memsaab shared with Raniya how she felt. And Raniya decided to quietly bury Chhoti Memsaab's regret in the depths of her heart. Some things are best left secret. Sometimes pain is best left unexpressed.

That day on returning to her neighbourhood after work, when Raniya went to wash up at the tap outside, she once again thought about Chhoti Memsaab's milky white feet. It must be the fault of her line of destiny that she inherited chapped and cracked feet while Chhoti Memsaab got beautiful, nail polish-adorned ones. With a toss of her head, she ejected the thought and splashed water on her eyes. Fields of flowers have no connection with the sky.

Chhoti Memsaab's stomach was swelling like a balloon, as was Ma's. Tending to both, Raniya's work kept increasing. A ten-minute delay, and her mobile phone would start ringing incessantly. Memsaab didn't let Chhoti Memsaab lift even a finger. Even her food was delivered to her bedside. Memsaab had even given Raniya strict instructions to wait outside the bathroom door. She had been relieved of all duties except those pertaining to the care of Chhoti Memsaab.

This was the first time Raniya had been given such an easy and light load in the house. But witnessing Chhoti Memsaab's boredom, waiting in silence for the days to pass and nights to fall – Raniya had never in her life taken on a heavier burden.

And then there was Ma, whose workload showed no sign of decreasing. She continued to go to her usual five houses to clean. That's why Raniya and her sister would head straight to the earthen stove as soon as they got home, so that Ma's burden would ease a bit. At least at home Raniya had respectable chores!

When Raniya told her exhausted mother to rest, Ma said, 'Arre, don't worry. I am used to giving birth while working.'

Sometimes, a mention of Chhoti Memsaab would slip out. 'The lines of destiny we were born with don't spell luxury, Raniya. I don't have the good fortune of your Chhoti Memsaab, to be able to lie in bed for nine months. And how often? This child isn't the result of prayer and pledge, unlike your Chhoti Memsaab's. Its very purpose is to lend a hand in our labours and struggles.' Ma pointed to her swollen belly and went back to rolling rotis.

Raniya thought to herself that perhaps the lines of destiny were formed in the womb itself. Lines of prayer and pledge. Lines that were broken and blown, criss-crossing and coming into being without reason.

A room had been rented for Chhoti Memsaab at the private nursing home of Noida's best doctor. She was admitted in the eighth month itself and Raniya's duties shifted there. She has a special vistor's badge. The first official document proving her service! She had never felt so special.

Who knew what fear ate the mistress that she spent all day praying and asking for boons, turning up in the evening with a big basket of prasad for Chhoti Memsaab. She didn't even scold or shout at anyone these days. One risked angering god incognito. Who knew whose form the great sage Durvasa might take? So that prayer and devotion would yield a grandson, she even went to the Bhairav Mandir at Pragati Maiden with bottles of rum, vowing to undertake a waterless fast for twenty-one Tuesdays.

Raniya often thought that having a child was not such a big deal! Her mother managed to give birth every couple of years.

Chhote Sahab had also taken leave from work and mostly stayed in hospital. He spent the whole day by his wife's bedside, tapping away on his phone. Sometimes he opened up his laptop too, but not often.

Raniya had never seen them fighting like her parents, but nor had she seen them talking much. Though they occupied the same room, they seemed very distant. Whatever it might be, be it through fights, Ma and Babu were making babies every two years, weren't they!

One evening, Raniya returned from the hospital and got scared on seeing an odd, drawn expression on Ma's face. Raniya's elder sister Sarita has gone to fetch Muniya's grandmother from next door.

Ma's face was darkening with pain. Raniya didn't know whether she should run out and get help or stay with Ma to keep her spirits up. She had never witnessed childbirth before. Only heard some bizarre stories from the elder women.

Raniya pressed Ma's right palm in her fist. She knew no other way of comforting.

In the throes of unconsciousness, Ma was mumbling something or the other.

'There's a clean dhoti at the bottom of the chest, bring it … heat water in the small cauldron … has your Babu not returned home … where has Sarita gone off to, she isn't back yet…'

After endless minutes and many screams, her sister Sarita entered from the back with Muniya's grandmother and Jenny Aunty from the neighbourhood. Jenny Aunty was a nurse. Maybe she could do something. The women ejected the girls from the room and started attending to Ma by themselves.

Sitting outside, Raniya kept listening to the strange noises and, at some point, as was her habit, dozed off and slumped down at the door itself.

A snakeling had emerged from Ma's stomach, wrapping itself around her chest, looking around at everyone and hissing venomously. Raniya was holding a small gold cane in her hands. She didn't want to get snake blood on it. Babu was yanking her plait. 'Why don't you raise your hand? What a fool you are, Raniya …'

Dulari Kaki was the one pulling at Raniya's braid and trying to wake her.

'How much you sleep, Raniya, you Kumbhkaran's sister! I've been yelling for an hour trying to wake you up. Go on inside. You have a brother. He's beautiful, with black forelocks and a complexion like a sahib … absolutely white. Arre, don't you understand what I'm saying? Why are you looking at me so? Go, go on inside. Take care of your mother, understand?'

Caught unawares, Raniya got up and went inside. After giving birth, Ma was relaxed, sleeping off Raniya's exhaustion. Beside her, swaddled in the white dhoti, her newborn brother looked around curiously with his round eyes. Raniya bent and observed him, before lying down next to him. The dream with the snake and the gold cane was lost somewhere.

Raniya woke up late. By that time, her mother had gone to the kitchen and was lighting the stove. Raniya's new brother was asleep, Babu was taking out the baskets of vegetables to take to work and Sarita held Chhotki as she swept the doorway, pushing out the dirt in the house to blend with that outside.

Washing up quickly, Raniya ran to the hospital to tend to Chhoti Memsaab. It had been a month and half of her staying there! That doctor was crazy! After seeing her mother give birth, her suspicion that the doctor was crazy had become even stronger.

It's not as if Chhoti Memsaab was sick, she was just having a baby. Then why all this fuss?

Then one day, Ramesh Uncle stopped her at the hospital's entrance. Uncle's face was dried up, his eyes red. On seeing Raniya, he said, 'Go home, Raniya. Chhoti Memsaab doesn't need you any longer.'

Shocked, Raniya kept looking at him and then, without saying anything, advanced towards Chhoti Memsaab's room. Raniya mused that perhaps along with Chhoti Memsaab's doctor, her driver Ramesh Uncle had also gone crazy!

Outside Chhoti Memsaab's room there was deathly silence. She was lying inside, without her bump. Chhote Sahab was discussing something with the doctor in the corridor while Memsaab sat on a chair with her eyes shut. Nobody noticed Raniya. Nobody asked her why she was late.

From behind her, Ramesh Uncle, come to deliver medicines, grabbed her hand and dragged her downstairs. 'But what has happened, Uncle? Chhoti Ma'am is sleeping in the room. Then why is everyone so upset? Was it a boy or a girl? I saw her belly...'

'A dead baby came out of her belly. You were looking after a dead baby all these days. Poor girl ... what terrible luck that woman has.'

A stunned Raniya tried to make sense of Ramesh Uncle's words.

'Dead babies don't come out of bellies, do they? This Ramesh Uncle blabbers nonsense. Out of Ma's belly had come my adorable little brother. I'll ask Chhoti Ma'am directly later. Right now the old man won't even let me go in.' With these thoughts Raniya exited the hospital.

In the afternoon once Ramesh Uncle had driven off homewards with Chhote Sahab and Badi Memsaab, Raniya swiftly went up to Chhoti Memsaab's room, taking the stairs by leaps and bounds.

On seeing her, Chhoti Memsaab coldly said, 'Go, Raniya. I don't need you. I don't even need myself.'

Raniya returned home. She didn't say anything to anyone, just sat with her newborn brother in her lap.

Dozing off while sitting, Raniya dreamt of Chhoti Memsaab in a sparkling red sari, holding a lifeless baby in a white cloth in her lap. Her brother's round kohl-lined eyes, Ma's swollen belly, Chhoti Memsaab's nail-polish-adorned toes, beds of blood-red flowers, broken and blown lines crisscrossed … in her sleep, they had all become tangled.

The Live-In

From Avi's Blog Drafts

26.12.2012

What a morning it was – hazy, cold and with sharp winds gusting. Naina's phone call woke me early in the morning. I can't tell you how annoyed I was. She commanded me to meet her at the gate in ten minutes and I heeded her! Not just that, but I abandoned the warm blanket and hot blower to go answer her summons. Not just that, but I brought her back upstairs. Baggage et al!

Naina had turned up without warning at my society's gate, belongings in tow. To live with me. I mean, to live in with me. Can you beat that?

Such was this morning I shared with Naina that for the first time in my life I felt the consequences of being accidentally cut by a double-edged sword. I mean, falling in love, having an affair and getting into a relationship is all very well. But a live-in?

Had Naina moved in with me in any month but December I might have been able to endure the relationship for a few more months. But does stubbornness ... that too, the stubbornness of a girlfriend ... that too, the stubbornness of a girlfriend ready to become a wife ... that too, the stubbornness of a girlfriend ready to live in before becoming a wife ... ever make sense that Naina's would?

The countdown begins.

From Naina's diary

26 December 2012

I have a fantasy. One that makes me want to close my eyes, lie down somewhere and die fantasizing. '*Teri baahon mein marr jaayein hum*...' the silly thought Simran had while melting into Raj's arms in that mustard field couldn't just have randomly struck her.

But this is no fantasy, it's reality.

Had I really had the guts to leave my hostel room and move in with Avi? To live in with him? I must be smoking something else!

But if I hadn't come to live in, what else could I have done? We're together day and night anyway – with each other even while in our own worlds. So then, what was the point of this listless distance?

Now when I toss and turn at night, I can touch your back, Avi. My fingers won't have to wait for an assignation to hold your palms. I won't have to rush back to the hostel, leaving your favourite mutton curry cooking slowly on the stove's low flame. I'll be able to have the morning coffee you make.

I can't write any more.

Stay with me. Stay with me always, Avi.

From Avi's Blog Drafts

30.12.2012

I was on my way to Lucknow on an office trip when I met a girl. It was a very 'Dharma Productions' style meet.

I noticed the girl sitting next to me when she asked, 'Can I borrow your pen please?' I swear on the life of all the world's beautiful girls that it's not in my nature to miss seeing one. But that day, my gaze didn't register the girl sitting right next to me almost until the Shatabdi reached Aligarh! (We were going to be co-passengers on the long journey of life, perhaps that's why.) By the way, for completely ignoring the girl who'd been sitting next to me for two hours, I throw the blame squarely at the feet of an individual called S.J. Watson. Had I not been eager to finish the last 89 pages of his thriller, I wouldn't have wasted those two hours.

'Can I borrow your pen, please?' The first time she asked disrupted my reading, the second time my thoughts. Though in the time she took to ask me twice I had already committed everything about her from eyes to the colour of her stole to my mind's Random Access Memory. She had almond eyes. Deep brown eyeliner applied above and below her lashes gave the impression of those almond eyes reaching her ears. The girl was beautiful. Very beautiful.

'You have one peeping out of your purse,' I said, intending to further conversation with this beautiful girl.

'This one doesn't work. It's a Cross pen only in name. Quite useless. Can I still borrow your pen?'

'Is this the latest pick-up line?' Close on the heels of the inappropriate words that left my mouth was the desire to give myself two tight slaps in front of everyone on the train. Maybe she hadn't heard me, or perhaps ignored it if she had; taking my pen she settled down to do a newspaper crossword.

Her handwriting was as clear as her voice – appearing like raindrops falling on the newspaper page. Out of the corner of my eye, I saw that it was my pen moving right and left between two tender fingers as though lost in deep thought. If it's true that handwriting is an indicator of character, this girl was a bit too honest. (And I was perfectly fine not getting to know her better!)

By the time we reached Tundla, she had solved the crossword, the sudoku, everything on the page, and I had devoured a thriller titled *Before I Go To Sleep*. Between Tundla and Itawa, our exchange had moved beyond the pen to the novel and by the time we pulled into Kanpur Central, we had moved beyond books and got to know a fair bit about each other's work. It's true that I learned her name 50 km before Lucknow, but what else could an almond-eyed girl be named but Naina?

Getting off at Lucknow, she extended her hand saying, 'It was nice meeting you', and I extended both my palm and pen, requesting her phone number. Using my pen, she inscribed her phone number in her clear handwriting on my palm for me and I kept memorizing it until the porter placed my luggage into the taxi.

The first meeting is like a favourite poem that we repeat loudly and find reasons to revisit. Once that meeting has been gilded with love, with a relationship, it becomes more like a tedious passage one is forced to memorize as part of fourth grade homework. This is what's happening to me, which is why I'm forgetting why, where and how many times Naina and I met after this.

I did indeed think many times during the ten months between our first meeting aboard the Lucknow Shatabdi and Naina coming to live-in with me that this love was the One (though never strongly enough that it'd reach the point of us moving in together, something to think about).

When it comes to love, I am impulsive, and Naina is even more impetuous than me – quite opposite to what her symmetrical handwriting suggests. It was this impetuousness and whimsicality that bound me to her. Her whimsicality exceeded life's boundaries. We met once in Lucknow and many times upon returning to Delhi. I'm not that old but there are ten years between thirty-three and twenty-three. Naina herself erased the ten-year difference ... from her end.

Living together would reveal the many differences between us, why didn't Naina understand this?

From Naina's diary

1 January 2013

It's the first day of the new year and my sixth in Avi's – our – house. Ma wanted to wish my roommate a happy new year. Stroking Avi's forehead as he slept, I told Ma that she was asleep.

The roommate is cross. She says I shouldn't have made such an impulsive decision. Truly, I ought not to make impulsive decisions. But Avi isn't an impulse, he's destiny's carefully hatched conspiracy. What else can account for this madcap move, within ten months, to leave everything behind and choose to forever be writing about him in my diary sitting at his very desk in his very house?

What love is, I don't know. But if it reduces you to the state I'm in, then love is wicked. It's even brought out the wickedness within me. After all, as far as my mother is concerned, I've become a liar and a fraud.

From Avi's Blog Drafts

2.1.2013

It has been barely a week since Naina and I started living together and I already wish I could leave Delhi and set up home on some snowy mountain – my house, for me alone. Or that I could take Naina by the hand and drag her to a peak near the moon and declare – this is the moment to take the leap of death, sweetheart! Will you be able to jump for my sake? Else if both of us survive, we shall be destroyed in the struggle to live our own lives.

How could I explain to Naina that being in such close quarters facilitated not unconditional love but selfish compromise! When apart, we thirst for each other, and this thirst propels a hunger for the other's taste. When together, we taste not each other but the poison inside ourselves that we keep picking at and releasing. The fear of losing Naina weighed so heavily on my mind that I wish to lose her forever. I wish to distance myself from her.

And on the other hand, there's Naina, who has traipsed in to live with a man like myself. I'd never imagined that our habit of meeting after work to have coffee together would lead us to this point.

The night that Naina, after the post-coffee dinner and post-dinner walk, returned not to her home but with me to mine, was the first night that I glimpsed her inner wellspring of impetuousness burst forth.

Doing the dishes at my sink in my kitchen I asked her, 'Where'll you tell your roommate you spent the night?'

'Why do I need to tell her anything?'

'What'll you tell your folk?'

'Why tell even them anything?'

'A thousand lies to hide one.'

'I just want to live authentically. A thousand lies are too few for that to happen.'

A slave to her impetuousness and oblivious to the running tap and half-scoured plate, Naina had breached my defences with the power of a merciless thunderstorm. Drowning in her impetuousness, I was witnessing with my own eyes the scene of my initial destruction.

From Avi's Blog Drafts

12.1.2013

The real problem started ever since Madam, in her trackpants and white jogging shoes, became determined to drag me out of my blanket early in the morning. Who goes for a morning walk in the cold January of Delhi! But Madam must go. That too, with me. Madam has begun to notice everything these days – my paunch, my overgrown beard, my greying hair, my dirty nails, my wet towel, my smelly socks.

I swear by Naina, these days I keep mentally screaming 'BREAAAKKKKUUPPPP!' If you want to wreck your life, there's no better way than love.

Today too, I circled the park fifteen times, but rebelled at the idea of stopping and having tea at the tea-stall at the turn of the alley.

'I don't drink tea. Definitely not on an empty stomach. Just seeing the tea boiling with these black leaves in the pan makes me want to throw up.' I put my point across as sensitively as I could.

'This is exactly why ... this was the very reason Avi ... it was important for us to live in. We still hardly know each other.' She extended the glass to me and I took it – less because of Naina's lecture and more with the intention of providing some warmth to my frosted hands.

It's because we hardly know each other that we're together. If we get to know each other too well, we'll separate, I wanted to tell her, but hadn't the nerve, the words stuck in my throat (and that's why I'm blogging about it; and that's why this post will remain in 'Drafts').

I am suddenly reminded today of Miss Alice, my high-school English teacher who, while teaching a Keki N.

Daruwalla poem, said in class, 'Every relationship comes with an expiry date.' The remarkable thing is that Miss Alice was teaching a love poem in class that day.

Her star-erasing beauty's spell,
turns me feverish, frail, unwell,
Her presence is both bliss and hell –
I tremble so.

I remember this poem by heart because in less time than it took Miss Alice to teach this poem, I had won over our class's most in-demand girl Aditi Banerjee by sending her notes with other Keki N. Daruwalla poems from a book I'd stolen from the library.

I also remember this poem by heart because 'Her star-erasing beauty's spell / turns me feverish, frail, unwell' are lines that I've used in every relationship, every affair, for every girl. No matter how often you love, it has the capacity to render a hale and hearty person frail and unwell. But we never learn our lesson for the next time. Consider it a manufacturing defect. And the remarkable thing is that some poet or other finds the words to accurately describe this weakness! In my next life, I want to be a poet – a bachelor poet, who is never bound to live in with anyone ever.

I had understood Miss Alice's statement right as a callow youth. Relationships are a means to an end. I'm unable to pass time, so I call you up to ease my restlessness.

I have nothing to do, so I email you, chat with you online. I was pointlessly stressed in life, so I asked you to spend an evening with me.

Each relationship is a means to an end, each relationship driven by some interest.

So, is Naina the muse for whom I might wish to collect and string together the scattered bits of myself divided by my heart? I'll have to think. But my inner compulsive bachelor is set on mutiny.

Naina and Avi's WhatsApp messages

25 January 2013

Naina: by when'll you return? i'll leave work in 10 mins.

Avi: i'll be late. very late. don't wait up. i have the spare key.

Naina: but i don't have a spare boyfriend!

Avi: ha ha ha. this was not funny Naina.

Naina: OK sorry. i love you Avi.

Naina: Avi

Naina: Avi

Naina: Avi if you don't reply, i'll call you right now.

Avi: Naina please. i'm trying to finish some work. are you home?

Naina: yeah, dinner?

Avi: not for me. good night.

Naina: then what's the point of living in Avi? for the past week now, you've been getting home past midnight.

Avi: it's the annual clearing. deadline. i'll talk tomorrow.

Naina: i don't want to talk.

Avi: thank god, you don't want to talk!

From Naina's diary

25 January 2013

I have to email my project report by eight o'clock tomorrow morning and my mind is blanker than a sheet of paper. I never thought I'd hate my first job this much. In what moment of insanity did I take up a bank job? Half the time rumours of a merger with some other bank do the rounds and the other half goes in goal-setting over email. Before this job has me kicked out of the company, I really want to be the one to kick this job aside.

But one does not simply quit a job, in the same way one doesn't quit love. It's a strange quandary. Naina Singh, who told you to undertake the taming of two deadly creatures at the tender age of twenty-three?

I have almost come to a decision. Ma keeps calling and droning about marriage. I'll muster the courage to tell her that I'm trying a live-in and the result of the live-in is that I'm gaining clarity about marriage.

Living at the hostel with a roommate was the right course of action. At least I didn't expect her to come home on time. Whatever this repressed passion inside me was, it was better left dormant. I don't know what Avi has done. I am not myself. And as far as the job is concerned, if it's just to pay rent that we work, I'll go off to a monastery some day, I swear!

Oh bravo, Naina Singh! Don't want to marry. Don't want to work. No existential purpose in sight. Sister Philomena must have suffered like me to have assumed nunhood one day. Lifelong abstinence – lifelong restraint ... temperance ... sacrifice. Lifelong escapism. How much courage does it take to run away? More than it takes to live in with someone?

I've been unable to get used to this house. Even now, within just two rooms of this house, in the dark I bump into walls, drawers, tables and chairs. The blue marks remain on my body. There are bruises everywhere and only one salve for each of them – Avi's feather-light touch.

It's almost two, and Avi still hasn't returned.

Naina and Avi's WhatsApp messages

12 February 2013

Naina: Avi, i've forgotten the key at home. please leave yours in the letterbox when leaving for work.

Avi: i won't go into work today, what say? will you eat mutton curry for lunch?

Naina: right now my boss is eating my brain. we'll have to skip it today.

Avi: show the middle finger to that idiot and come home.

Naina: please Avi. just because your deadline is past, anything goes?

Avi: alright, sorry. at least you'll come home early?

Naina: it's your turn to wait now. I spent the entire week waiting up, Avi.

Avi: are you this vindictive? you'll exact revenge?

Naina: had we not lived in, how would you come to know this about me, Avi?

Avi: every moment of getting to know you is no less than a treasure hunt. you're a mysterious woman, Naina.

Avi: Naina…

Avi: Naina…

Avi: Naina, please reply to this message else i'll come down to your office.

From Avi's Blog Drafts

14.2.2013

Living with Naina, I've understood this much about myself – I am an existentially bored loner at heart. Having survived fifteen or sixteen relationships by the age of thirty-three, I've ceased my quest for peace and happiness.

The questions raised when I'd run away to the city ten years ago have died down, leaving no reason for me to marry and settle down.

Many people have tried to break into my life. By people I mean girls. But until now nobody had taken over my sense of self with Naina's confidence. One may call it the wisdom that comes with age. Maybe, like women, men too have a biological clock. (Men? When had I become aware of having grown from a boy into a man?)

Every day when I pant while running, Naina is the only one with the capacity to tolerate my frustration, depression, madness and self-destruction. She has aged ten years living in with me. I've regressed into a ten-year-old living in with her. The branch of love that my inner woodcutter had decided to axe down was freshly abud, since when? Wasn't its time up?

'Her presence is both bliss and hell – I tremble so…'

In my memory are drawn-out tales of love. Like a three-act play, these tales map onto a pattern of beginning, middle and end, but have no resolution. I kept falling in love with whomever I met in whichever state. I had no definition, no milestone, nor any model of love to emulate. When all our lives we see people being distant even when together, we can't understand love in its successful form. Whatever else these unresolved tales might be, they were very important to me. I'd learnt to emerge from regret thanks to those tales. And then there's Naina, who despite living with my disaffection and eccentricity, gives me reasons to live.

Valentine's Day is being celebrated all over the world today. The day of commodifying and marketing love. I too am off to do this. Arranging dinner for Naina is less a matter of desire and more one of necessity. Selfish compromises, so that no matter what, we avoid a row. One of the biggest dangers of living in – selfish compromises. I'm scared of seeing the reflection in the mirror held up by these compromises.

Why have I started to change so much?

'Her presence is both bliss and hell – I tremble so…'

Naina and Avi's WhatsApp messages

28 February 2013

Naina: hi Avi, i'm crashing with my roommate tonight. in in my hostel room.

Avi: why?

Naina: i need some 'me time'. i'm craving a pyjama party and hanging out with girls my own age.

Avi: what do you mean? that i'm not your age?

Naina: i didn't mean that Avi. it's just that i'm missing my friends.

Avi: and what about me missing you?

Naina: Avi, it's just one night.

Avi: the tsunami came ashore in a night. a night's rain nearly drowned Mumbai. for life to change, even a moment, forget a night, is enough.

Naina: doesn't Android have an emoji for hitting one's head against a wall? Avi, you're taking it too far now.

Avi: ok go. but i'll miss you.

Naina: no i'm not going anywhere. save some food for me please.

Avi: where's the kiss emoji?

Naina: you have lost it Avi. bye. see you.

Avi: come soon.

From Naina's diary

5 March 2013

Avi says my restlessness is a clinical condition. Even if Avi hadn't said as much, I'd figured this out. How can those born to wander alter their genetic structure, after all! It's not as if Avi had changed that I could!

Until now, it was this impetuousness, this restlessness of mine that kept Avi bound to me. Now he keeps finding fault with these very qualities. If this is a live in, what's marriage? A requirement to have children? I've started speaking Avi's language and he mine. This is one of the biggest dangers of living in.

Well, there's no resolution to this monologue in my own diary. I have no control over what I keep thinking these days. Three close friends have been searching for jobs over the past two months. I'm serving out my notice period. My banking career looks like it's kaput before it begins. I don't even know up to what point I'll accompany Avi. How could I even find peace? Sometimes I think of becoming a yoga instructor. Other times I consider returning to Lucknow and becoming a teacher in some small school. Occasionally I think I should listen to Ma and get married – not to Avi, but to some normal person who'll give me normal children. For whom I'd spend half my life cooking and wiping the noses of our kids. Who are those women who live in peace?

I'm going home today. There are a thousand errands to run before that – at home, outside. I have to pack, finish some bank work. Fulfil false promises made to friends. The morning walk can't be given up on, and who'll fill in for me at the bank? Despite my best efforts, I remain disorganized, the power notes glisten on the screen uselessly and the time management guides I read during MBA preparation taunt me. Time management is still possible, but mind management? Or heart management?

Dried neem leaves are falling effortlessly onto the windscreen of a car parked in the lot, far from the windowsill

I'm sitting and writing my diary at. The sunshine is playing peekaboo and autumn is at its most nubile. In the distance is the horizon where nothing is visible but an endless road. Before embarking on my journey home, I sit, tired. Abida Parveen sings something on Avi's music system.

Reminiscing about these fleeting moments of peace is actually the calm before the storm. Well, our accord was to remain in discord, Avi. Why had I met you at all on the Lucknow Shatabdi?

Naina and Avi's WhatsApp messages

4 April 2013

Avi: Naina, when'll you get back? you've been gone for more than a month.

Naina: i don't have a job Avi. what do i have to return for?

Avi: you have me. return and you'll see. we'll combine forces to get you a second break. better than the first time.

Naina: the first time is never good. not even first love.

Avi: what are you getting at Naina?

Naina: you tell me Avi. you're more experienced in matters of love. are these the signs of a break-up?

Avi: no these are the signs of you losing it. come back. for your mental health it's important that someone grab you and kiss you long and hard.

Naina: someone?

Avi: obviously … me.

Naina: Avi can i ask you something? will you tell me?

Avi: ask away Naina.

Naina: how is kiss 'a' different from kiss 'b' and 'c'?

Avi: what sort of an absurd question is this Naina? you really need to come back. to me.

Avi: Naina...

Avi: Naina why aren't you responding? at least take my calls.

Avi: Naina if you don't reply i'll come to Lucknow. i don't want to live in. i want to marry you.

From Naina's diary

15 May 2013

I don't know what's got into me. I've started lying to the very Avi that I had lied so much for. This is not for me. This is absolutely not for me. How is marriage possible when a live-in wasn't?

How can I admit that ever since I returned to Lucknow – in this inconstant weather with its humid nights and molten-ice cream days, Avi's touch has started to feel not cool but cold. Do relationships run their course so quickly? Ma's right. This Instant Message generation doesn't know how to wait. This Instant Message generation doesn't know how to love either.

I bump into the walls of this house too, but on purpose. I've started to feel smothered. It's possible that this is because of my own failures. It's also possible that I'm bored. It's also possible that I've begun to fear commitment. It's also possible that I've started to change. It's also possible that I've completely lost my marbles…

Avi was right, love really is the biggest asshole!

From Avi's Blog Drafts

30.5.2013

I used to cross a wooden bridge to get to school. At the Central School in Aizawl, few kids spoke Hindi. I don't know how many such Central Schools I studied at. I don't know how many friends I made and how many I left behind. A government servant's children never belong to any city, nor any friend or school. And if that government servant doesn't even belong to their family, God save their children.

I've lived with many strangers. All of them led me to believe that whomever you love, they will belong to you. I learned well to love others. Learned well to love myself through others. I made others my own, those parts of them that suited my nature. The day my reflection in the mirrors they held up started to blur, I stopped loving them. That's why I could never belong to anyone. Perhaps because something was left lacking in my lessons as a child.

I couldn't belong to Naina either. In spite of wanting to. I recall all those faces that had belonged to me. I recall the reasons behind getting involved and the rationale behind the disentanglements even. The alacrity with which we find causes to connect with others matches that with which we find reasons to separate from them. This time, the excuses and reasons are all Naina's finds. Naina is the atonement for my sins.

Naina had asked what difference her departure would make. She had come to stay of her free will. She was leaving of her free will too. Naina truly didn't care that her being here shielded me from a hundred scourges. All the mornings begun with her were devoid of complaints.

I left the house to shelter under a sheet spun with wanton and carefree moments. In all these years under that sheet, I'd never thought about the bodies with whom I shared my restlessness. Naina taught me to introspect. Maybe she didn't like what I'd tried to teach her. Truly, we shouldn't have met on the Lucknow Shatabdi. I should have taken Naina back to her home the very day she came over to live in with me. Had we stayed apart, we might have sustained our intimacy for longer. If marriage is the world's most obscene institution, then live-ins are the biggest cause of relationships imploding.

Today, I feel like murdering both Miss Alice and Keki N. Daruwalla.

Co-Passengers

I was to board the train at Badnera station. This train was the best one to get to Ahmedabad by. The Puri–Ahmedabad Express. I would reach by seven in the morning, making it possible to work all day and reach Delhi by the evening Rajdhani.

I had come to Amravati for the shooting of a documentary film. I had my camera – a DSR 450. A boon for a cameraperson like myself. Not too heavy, and the shoot quality was similar to the Digi Beta. It's not that I didn't want to pick up a heavy camera, but a frail frame of five-foot two-inches has its limits. On an average, I am athletic. I can pick up anything and take off anywhere. But for the past few months, spondylitis had kept gripping my neck again and again. And so, I was forced to bear a small camera and an excessively kooky assistant. This time, too, Vijay was with me.

The train stopped for only two minutes at Badnera station and so, handing over the responsibility of the monitor and tripod to Vijay, I stood waiting for the bogey a full ten minutes in advance. Vijay wanted to sit but as the 'cameraman', I was the boss. Bag strapped to my back. Camera slung on my shoulder. Water bottles and biscuit packets in both hands. I'd even managed to squeeze a newspaper under my arm. My hands were busy, my mind long habituated to being burdened while walking.

But something had happened to Vijay today – he was in the mood to enjoy the trip to the fullest.

'There's still time for the train, ma'am. Shall we have tea?' Without waiting for my response, he left the luggage beside me and went off to the tea stall.

For some reason, I didn't feel like sitting anywhere. For one, the iron chairs were spaced out and besides, this was a convenient spot. The bogey would pull up right here and the TV mounted on the platform was visible too, currently playing *Chitrahaar*-type songs. First it was a song sequence from a Sanjeev Kumar-Shabana Azmi film, and now the screen showed Zeenat Aman and Amitabh Bachchan standing entwined. I couldn't hear the lyrics but seeing the videos caused, through force of habit, the film songs to echo in my mind one after the other.

Leaving Delhi, you realize that small towns deliberately arrest themselves in nostalgia. This nostalgia and these retro songs playing on the TV and radio are a collective coping mechanism to protect themselves from dull days and still nights. I too wanted to live this nostalgia for a bit longer.

Getting up from here would mean taking the trouble to shift and settle the luggage as well as giving up what little entertainment was available on the TV screen.

Vijay had brought tea, accompanied by onion pakodas. Had I not glimpsed flies swarming on the pakodas decorating the stall on my way to the platform, I might have taken the whole lot from Vijay. As it was, I stuffed into the bag the biscuit packets and water bottles I held in my hands and took the tea he offered.

The train had been announced. We were the only two passengers to board the 2 AC coach from here. In any case, who'd want to travel in this scorching heat!

The train arrived. Seat no. 1 of the first compartment in 2 AC. Vijay had been allotted seat no. 38. There are many disadvantages to boarding long-distance trains at nondescript stations. Firstly, there's no way you'll get a seat of your choice. Secondly, between the long-distance co-passengers sprawled on their seats and their heavy-duty bags and boxes, it's impossible to arrange your luggage. Thirdly, dirty toilets.

As the third disadvantage occurred to me, my mind spun. Both the lower berths were already under occupation. I was faced with the prospect of dealing with all three disadvantages of boarding trains from nondescript stations.

From behind a white sheet, a wizened face emerged, one on which it appeared as though after the age of seventy-five, both body and mind had ceased to annually twist the strands extending the rope of Age. From amidst his wrinkles, the toothless Uncle smiled, 'I won't be able to climb up. Daughter, do you mind exchanging seats?'

Because he was toothless, it was the gestures of his hands, more than the Marathi-Gujarati words from his mouth that conveyed the request. The approximately thirty-five-year-old woman lying on the lower berth opposite didn't consider it worthwhile to raise her head from her book, nor to take the trouble of clearing some space for me under her seat, amid the slippers, bags, newspaper pages and plates scattered there. I knew at once that women like this were the ones who took undue advantage of the woman card. I was overcome with vexation regarding my age and gender.

I stood with my camera still slung on my shoulder in exactly the same pose I'd been in on the platform when the train arrived. A bag strapped to my back. Water bottles and biscuit packets in both hands. And spondylitis slowly tightening its hold on my neck.

'Sure, I'll exchange seats. But why don't you ask this lady to make some room for me?' I said, agitatedly.

'We aren't travelling together.' A cool voice carried from behind the book, but even so she didn't make any effort to get up and manage her things.

My temper flared. I used my feet to forcefully shove her slippers and plate of leftovers towards the coach's aisle. Madam continued to read, indifferent to my kick. Just a slight movement of feet under her blanket. But her eyes stayed on the book. I'd caught the book's title: *Premashram*. Huh! Who else but Premchand would women who only buy books at railway platforms read?

Annoyed, I started pulling out the baggage from under the berth. But how to manage? The bags were fastened using an iron chain.

'Do you mind gathering your things or shall I throw them off the train?'

Despite my harsh tone, the woman didn't move. On the contrary, she hit back, 'How do you have the right to do that? There's ample room under the other seat, can't you see?'

'I can't. I see only rudeness. It's five-thirty in the evening. Is this a time to be lying down? You didn't even bother to move your feet enough to make place for your co-passenger. And Uncle, you. Yes, hello. Uncle, I'm talking to you. You may absolutely take the lower berth. But at least for the next three hours, give me room to sit.'

The old gent got up in a flurry. I threw the water bottles and biscuit packets onto the seat with such force that you could hear the sound of biscuits crumbling inside the packet. I was angry enough to shove the woman sprawled on the seat as well. But my agitation had no effect on her and she continued lying there, reading her book. I too disappeared behind a newspaper, but my mental monologue didn't end.

'Goodness knows what these folks think of themselves! One seat reserved and it's as if the entire train is their property. An utter lack of civic sense. Litter where you eat. No doubt servants are expected to pick up slippers and bags. Reading *Premashram* and considering yourself an intellectual. If you must read Premchand, read *Godaan*, read *Gaban*, read *Rangbhumi*, read *Karmbhumi*. Read his short stories. Reading *Premashram*. Probably couldn't find anything else at the station's bookshop. More likely didn't understand whatever was available. Her majesty must have seen the name Premchand and picked up the book, why not,' I ranted in my head.

'Have a thapela?' The toothless Uncle suddenly asked me and, in a hasty moment, I reluctantly took a piece from his tiffin box.

Taking that thapela cost me dearly. It was as if Uncle had been lying in wait for an opportunity. The key to the chatterbox had been turned.

'My name is J.P. Ghoghari, Jayprakash Ghoghari. I'm from Yavatmal, heading to Ahmedabad, to visit my son and daughter-in-law. Though I'm Gujarati, my people have been living in Yavatmal for about a hundred years. Where are you from, daughter?'

'I'm from Odisha,' I answered shortly. Any more would only encourage conversation, which I didn't want at all.

'From Odisha? Are you sure you haven't boarded the train in the opposite direction? This train goes from Puri to Ahmedabad, not from Ahmedabad to Puri.'

'I know.' I gritted my teeth. 'Ahmedabad.'

'Are you working?'

There it was. The question that irritates me no end. What does it meant to be working? Do housewives not work?

'What do you do?'

Ghoghori Uncle was extracting to the full the value of that morsel of thapela. But his eyes were fixed so intently on my face in anticipation of an answer that I didn't have the option to remain silent.

'I am a cameraperson. I … uh … take photos and videos. For TV.'

'Oh! You're a cinematographer in Delhi. This is what's so special about our nation. We belong to one place, settle someplace else. Not like the Americans; there, folk from the East Coast have probably never even seen the West Coast. Take me, for example. I'm Gujarati, born and brought up in Maharashtra. Worked all my life in Delhi and now living in Nagpur after retirement, with my elder son. Right now, I'm going to Ahmedabad to visit my younger son.'

Adopting a distant tone, I nodded and muttered, 'I see.'

But Mr Ghoghari's jabbering drone didn't stop.

'I'm from a family of freedom fighters and social reformers. You won't have seen a Gujarati family like ours.

Living in Maharashtra, we left no stone unturned to absorb Marathi culture. Do you know Gopalkrishna Gokhale?'

'Yes sir, I do. I've read about him in history books.' I still wasn't able to comprehend why I was not only listening to his prattle but giving him opportunities to keep talking.

Abruptly, I recalled the books queued up in my Kindle. So much to read – Marquez, William Dalrymple, James Patterson and a Nigerian writer whose name I couldn't recall just then.

'Indeed. You must have read about him. Gokhale was a great man. He was a close friend of my grandfather's. Do you know, my grandfather was the principal of Yavatmal Medical School. When Gokhale died in 1915, he organized a condolence meeting at his school. For this reason, the British fired and jailed him. But my grandmother didn't lose hope. Forget the school, she organized a condolence meeting in her village. It was an open challenge to the British. Let's see how many you're able to jail. Dadi would tell us that 250 women from the village convened. Never before had such a gathering of women been seen or heard of.'

'Hmm.' Abruptly, I recalled the Nigerian writer's name. Adichie, Chimamanda Ngozi Adichie. God knew if I had got the name right, but her feminist writing had stirred even a mulish person like myself. I had barely extended my hand to reach into my bag for the book before Ghoghori Uncle stopped me midway.

'Oh, do sit back down, daughter. Do you know, they say Mr Gokhale died of stress? Of tension. He died at quite a young age; is forty-nine an age to die?'

'Did people die of stress a hundred years ago?' My tone was sarcastic.

'How could he have avoided stress? The nation was enslaved. How much atrocity can you see inflicted on those around you, your family, community and nation? If you're even slightly compassionate, you'll be troubled by it. Tension is inevitable.' The supine woman in front of me spoke in a rush.

I had no reply to this unexpected response.

Ghoghori Uncle kept up the flow of conversation. How his father had dived into the independence struggle as a mere schoolboy. How, on hearing rumours of his grandfather's house's impoundment, his grandmother hid the entire family of eight children in the neighbour's stable and herself came to argue with the subedar – that too in Marathi. How his childhood was spent listening to and composing patriotic songs about freedom and how living to see seventy years of an independent India filled him with emotion. Only one thing gave me pause – Uncle was not seventy, but at least eighty years old!

Despite this realization, I was yet the disinterested audience, contributing no more than the occasional 'hmm'. But the woman, all the while reclining, conversed warmly with Ghoghori Uncle, as though they'd been friends for years.

The train reached Bhusaval at about ten. I still hadn't eaten anything and started to disembark with the intention of finding some food when I thought of Vijay. Engrossed in this deep conversation, I had almost forgotten about him.

As I got up, the woman addressed me in Odia, '*Train roo olihabe ki? Mo paain paanir bottle aanibe ki*?' Are you getting off? Do you mind getting me a bottle of water?

'How did you know that I speak Odia?' I asked, astonished.

'Didn't you tell the Uncle sitting opposite that you're from Odisha?'

'Oho! So, you were only pretending to read. Your attention was in fact on our conversation.' I retreated to irony.

The woman didn't respond. Turned around and lay down. I became vexed with myself. Why couldn't I control my damn tongue? It had a bad habit of slipping and spewing venom. But I didn't have the nerve to apologize either.

Turning to Uncle, I asked, 'Do you need anything?' Uncle declined with a gesture.

With a heavy heart, I alighted onto the platform. I didn't feel like eating anything. Packing some food for

Vijay, I was starting to board the coach through the other door when my eyes fell on the passenger list. The name of the woman opposite was Sushmita Panigrahi and she was twenty-eight years old. That made her a bit younger than myself. I didn't know whether to be annoyed with her or regret being annoyed with her. And so, handing Vijay the packet of food, I returned to stroll on the platform.

It did cross my mind once to apologize. But pride blocked the entrance to the coach with a thick barrier. Difficult to step over, impossible to bend down and pass. To distract myself from this dilemma, I kept taking deep drags of my cigarette. Why do people try to forge lifelong relationships over a one-night train journey? I mean, fine, chance decreed that we were all seated next to each other in one bogey but that didn't mean we should cling to one another. If clinging to co-passengers was undesirable, then why was I obsessing over my co-passengers' behaviour or mine towards them? Whoever Ghoghori Uncle was, or that woman who wanted to develop a rapport based on Odia, my interaction with them was limited to today – to this journey. With this thought, I lit another cigarette, despite the stares. I suddenly felt lighter. Why take on the burden of piercing looks from others?

The train having been signalled to proceed, I returned to the coach with a water bottle to find that both my co-passengers had switched off the lights and gone to sleep. Placing one water bottle on the table in front of the passenger named Sushmita Panigrahi, I uncapped the other bottle. Swallowing a muscle relaxant with a big gulp of water, I tried to apply a relief balm on my neck and upper back. Then lying on the upper berth, I switched on the reading light and tried unsuccessfully to read Adichie before nodding off.

The silence in the compartment, the noisy movement of the train on the tracks and the rumble of Ghoghori Uncle's snores pushed my mind towards a game of hide and seek again.

This was the very train aboard which I'd met Shalini.

One journey. Bonds aren't forged over merely one journey. We don't ever again bump into the people we meet on trains. As the journey comes to an end, so do the friendships as well as the random conversations. But my friendship with Shalini had started aboard this very train. And that relationship had shattered during life's long journey. By then, Shalini had inflicted a lot of pain on me. In the eight months between meeting and separating, we had lived together as flatmates and grown apart. Even now we wandered around with a thousand complaints in our hearts.

After that, I travelled many times by train but never struck up a friendship. Forget friendship, I never even struck up a conversation. Whenever I boarded a train, the brusqueness of my personality reached the point of insensitivity. Against my will.

When I awoke in the morning, the train was about to reach Ahmedabad. Passengers were starting to collect their belongings. Ghoghori Uncle too was stowing his slippers into his bag. I got down and started putting on my shoes as well. I didn't feel the need to speak to anyone. The woman on the opposite seat kept sleeping, facing the other away. Like two good co-passengers we had forgotten our behaviour towards each other.

No sooner did the train pull into Ahmedabad than along with the porters, a man in his mid-twenties burst into the compartment and stopped beside the woman lying opposite us.

'*Didi, didi … tumo phone baund kaahi ke ochhi? Mu bahut somoyo ru cheshta koruchhi?*' I was so worried. You could have kept the phone switched on at least.

'No re, the battery died. That's why it was switched off. If only I could reach the power point to charge it.' For the first time in fourteen hours, I noticed a beam of a smile on the woman's face.

'You could have asked for help. Requested your co-passengers.' The brother's voice still contained a note of anxiety.

'I don't have the right, nor is it a custom to ask co-passengers any more.' This time, it was the woman's voice that was ironic.

All this while, the brother kept dragging out the luggage and putting it on the seat. Along with the bags were a wheelchair and a pair of crutches. After taking out the luggage, he helped his sister sit up and that's when I realized that the woman had a prosthetic limb instead of a right leg.

I don't know why but I felt that I was being drenched with litres of water. I was able to meet neither Sushmita's gaze nor Ghoghori Uncle's. Even as he placed his on my head to bless me, my mind was on the wheelchair. With the help of a porter, the brother carried out the pieces of luggage one by one, then helped his sister down and into the wheelchair.

With a heavy heart, I kept sitting. I recalled and repeated like a refrain the two lines I'd read on the London Underground a month and a half before Vijay joined me. 'Even if you are trying to be polite / Try not to make space too tight.'

It was true what they said about taking a train journey with someone if you want to know their character and temper. That day, after the Puri–Ahmedabad Express journey, it suddenly dawned on me why Shalini might have left me.

And why, while collecting her things from the flat, she might have said, 'One who cannot see another person beyond her own sorrow can be neither a good friend, nor a good flatmate.'

Please Do Not Disturb

'Sleep here every day?'

Surely this wasn't the first question one asked.

But this was Mumbai, and nobody had the time to build background for conversation. In Mumbai, any question could be your first. Or last.

In any case, after asking the question Rohini more or less melted into the red sofa in the corner of the reception and closed her eyes, without waiting for an answer. Rohit couldn't think of anything to say. With her tight jeans and half-sleeve top, it was tough to guess Rohini's age. She could've been thirty-five or twenty-five. Age has nothing to do with clothes. In fact, age has nothing to do with complexion, disposition, habits … nothing to do with any of these things.

Living in Mumbai, Rohit was beginning to understand these unwritten, unspoken rules.

Boss had directed Rohit to pull a night shift, with the promise of a double holiday on Tue-Wed. A boss's promise of leave is no less dangerous than that made by a lover. Trouble if kept, catastrophe if not.

Anyway, Boss was unlikely to keep his promise and Rohit didn't see much harm in that. He didn't want to miss any opportunity to stay back in the studio. Not only would he be relieved of the humid heat of July, but he also needed to get used to night shifts. He had to make assistant editor in two years, editor in five. Impossible without slogging in the studio day and night.

'You're still up?' Rohini had awoken again. 'My editor's dozed off re. Nothing for me to do. Let's go to Lokhandwala Crossing and get cigarettes.'

Rohit's eyes automatically swivelled to the tick-tocking square clock on the far wall.

'New here or what? You know na, time's got no meaning here. If you're too chicken, I'll only go. Stay here, *darpok*. If my editor wakes, tell him I'll be back in fifteen.'

'No ma'am. I'll accompany you. How'll you manage alone?'

'Are you Salman Khan or what that you'll be my bodyguard?'

'No ma'am, I just meant ...'

'You ate something or just loafing about here? It's nearly two-thirty. And if you're hungry, there's *vada-pao* downstairs.'

'I've eaten, ma'am.'

'Then go upstairs and tell that horse we'll be back in ten minutes. This night duty business is a full waste. Not like work gets done, and it screws with your damn sleep.'

'Yes, ma'am.'

'You get here direct from Lucknow, or what? Keep talking like that and they'll make mincemeat of you, put you in the deep freezer and enjoy from time to time. Now run upstairs and tell him. We'll go loaf a bit.' Rohini rolled over on the sofa again.

Climbing up the stairs, he glanced at Rohini a few times. Would she really go out so late at night?

Upstairs in the edit suite, the editor was sleeping like a log that had long been detached from its tree. In fact, the sawing was so loud in the form of snores that it could be heard outside the soundproof room. The timeline lay listless on the FCP, as though it too needed a pick-me-up like Cinkara tonic … or perhaps a smoke.

This film will get smoked, that's what Boss had said just yesterday. It needed to be said. The very first shot was so dull! Rohit suddenly recalled that first shot, the hero swaggering out of a room. No innovation, neither in the shot nor in the edit…

Rohit played the timeline. Not even four scenes had been edited since yesterday. What exactly did they accomplish, pulling these night shifts? How could it take this long to edit a scene?

Seeing the randomness of the shots, he itched for a while to arrange them in a systematic sequence. Then he remembered Boss's instructions to not interfere in anyone else's work, and retreated to a corner.

Despite waiting for a bit, he was unable to decide whether to wake up the editor or go back downstairs. There was also the option of retrieving the key and locking the studio from outside. Even if the editor awoke, he'd call Rohini. Though looking at him, it didn't seem as though his body would do much apart from exhaling and inhaling noisily for the next two hours. Yama, the god of death himself, would probably beat a hasty retreat.

Locking the studio, Rohit trailed behind Rohini. That way, he'd avoid both the cigarette smoke and the punishment that was conversation with her.

After descending the stairs from the fourth floor, they would have turned towards Lokhandwala Crossing, but Rohini plopped down on the footpath. Rohit continued standing, studying the movements of her body with an uncertain gaze.

With her right hand, Rohini rolled up her left sleeve up to her shoulder, then stared at the cigarette box in her left hand for a long moment. With the fingers of her right hand, she took out a cigarette, tapped it against the box thrice, extracted a lighter from her jeans pocket and, lighting the cigarette up with a deep drag, settled back down…

Taking deep drags of the cigarette. Lost in deep thought.

'Where are you from, re?' Rohini's unexpected question broke into Rohit's reverie, and he anxiously looked towards the road.

'I asked where are you from? You don't look like you're from Bombay.'

'Yes ma'am, from Allahabad.'

'Ran away from home?'

'Sorry? No, ma'am.'

'Then you must've had a fight.'

Rohit lowered his eyes.

'What's there to feel guilty about? You only make it in Bombay if you run away to come here. Have a smoke?' Rohit shook his head to decline. Only a few moments are enough to fall prey to an addiction. Even a lifetime was too short to guard against bad habits.

'I ran away too. Not from too far. From nearby, Ratlam. Took a direct train on the Western Railways. Came here to be a film heroine, and now look what I've become.'

'By the way sister, what is it you do?'

'Made up a relation in ten minutes, eh? You're a clever one. Only, you make up the wrong relations.' At Rohini's words, Rohit flushed and, taking two steps back, resumed trying to identify the models of cars at the petrol station.

'Got a girlfriend?'

'Sorry?'

'Girlfriend? In Allahabad?'

'Yes ma'am, I have one.'

'Good. Means you have a reason to live. You want to know what I do, ask me what I *don't* do.'

'Sorry?'

'Not everyone's got Kangana Ranaut's luck. How do I look, re?'

'Sorry?'

'Sorry … yes ma'am … no ma'am … these the only English words you know?'

'No, ma'am … I mean … I know more than that.'

'So, tell me in English, how do I look?'

'Er … beautiful.'

'That's it? Drop a couple more words here.'

'Pretty … um … lovely … um …'

'Use the word "sexy", re, "sexy". Too shy to say it, or what? Say, "you look like a sex bomb".'

'Yes ma'am, that.'

'You're hopeless, re. How did you chat up your girlfriend?'

'Oh that? We just fell in love.' Thoughts of Latika had Rohit smiling unconsciously.

Rohini's guffaw once again plonked him down on the hard surface of Link Road.

'You're a spring chicken. There's time yet for your slaughter. Anyway, I came here to be a heroine but now I do everything. Whatever's needed. Pre-production, post-production, production control, and I can even set up a casting couch. These production guys gave me such a hard time that I figured I'd get into production and fuck them up. I'm getting my own back now. My cussing doesn't scare you, does it?'

'No ma'am, people use swear words where I'm from as well. It's not considered acceptable at home though.'

'Wasn't accepted at mine either. Left behind good manners when I left home. You'll also learn, damn soon. Come, I'll buy you coffee at Barista.'

'Ma'am, I don't drink coffee.'

'What do you do in life, apart from being in love?'

'I'm learning editing.'

'Learn, learn. Tell me when you need work. I'll get you jobs. Without favours. I like you.'

'It'll take me time to get there. I'm still getting a hang of the basics.'

'Where's your confidence, re? Say you'll do it all. That's how you get work. Haven't you seen my editor? He can't get one damn shot right on his own. You leave him be and he'll complete a two-shift edit in fifteen days. I sit on his head to get the job done. Good thing he has a goddamn pretty face, else I'd be ruining my sleep for nothing.'

'Sorry?'

'What for? Didn't you know he's my boyfriend? Ever saw anyone from production sit on an edit? You really do need time to get a hang. Your basics aren't even solid re.'

At the mention of the boyfriend, the sound of powerful snores returned to Rohit's ears. He was in such a deep state of shock that it felt as though his tongue was perhaps stuck to his palate and before his eyes appeared the 'Do Not Disturb' sign that had swung outside the edit suite the previous night.

With the same bindaas attitude with which that sign had probably been hung outside the edit suite, Rohini now smoked her third cigarette.

Life the Pain, Life the Cure

Shivani was in a strange dilemma. At times she wanted to visit her gynaecologist as though she alone could treat all malaises, at other times she avoided meeting Dr Shergill badly enough to consider switching doctors.

But a woman's relationship with her gynaecologist was like that romance that took mere months to blossom but years to forget.

Not only was Dr Gagdeep Shergill a lady doctor, she was also the unofficial doctor of Shivani's feelings. That was why, apart from periods, pregnancy, fibroids and PMS, she was able to diagnose the incurable afflictions circumambulating Shivani's heart in a snap, without so much as feeling a pulse.

How a doctor's gaze could X-ray her mind sometimes! One look at Dr Shergill's soft, liquid eyes and you'd understand how. For Shivani, lying to the gynaecologist was impossible and speaking the truth intolerable.

She was a doctor after all. She'd ask about symptoms, then check the pulse and then, fixing her spectacles atop her nose, she'd write in her fluent cursive handwriting all manner of this and that, straight and slant, nonsensical, who-knew-what, and hand Shivani the note.

Even more complicated than her disease was Doctor sahiba's note!

How she understood the state of Shivani's heart without a stethoscope. How she guessed her blood pressure just by looking at the complexion of her face. Doctor sahiba's blunt and direct questions would trouble Shivani in the same manner as her pointless thoughts.

Still, Shivani often found it necessary to plumb and pour out the depths of her heart to Dr Shergill, along with her body's aches and pains.

Something of this sort happened on the morning of 23 September.

As it was, Shivani had no reason to remember the date. But we do lots of things without reason, daily! From being born to going to school to attending college to marrying – it's all without reason. Having been born, one was forced to go through the motions and rituals of life, otherwise Shivani didn't see any purpose to getting through each day. She went on doing meaningless things. From leaving the bed each morning to sharing it with her husband each night.

It was all meaningless. Life was meaningless.

She'd come to consult regarding one illness and was picking at the wounds inflicted by another. Else, what was the connection between periods delayed by months and the heart's bruises?

'Oh, you idiot girl! Off with you! What's happened to you? This is a disease of the mind, not your uterus.' When she was cross, Dr Shergill's Punjabi-ness seeped into her accent. At such moments, she was no longer a doctor, but a woman.

It was this woman that Shivani went to meet each time.

'All illnesses are of the heart. You're a doctor, who'd know more about psychosomatic disorders than you?'

'A psychiatrist. Go check your foolish self into a mental institution! Your brains have been addled and I've been saying this since before you knew what the full form of IVF was.'

'Not addled, my brain's now healthy. Do you remember, Doctor, how aimlessly I'd spend my days back then? I'd wait each month for my periods not to come. Now I want to hold onto time, as well as to the woman in me. Now that I'm aware, I think about how life has passed me by and the rabbit never came out of the magician's hat. I never got the chance to hold a bouquet of colourful plastic flowers. The umbrella above my head never changed colours. The magician just passed a double-edged sword through me. What kind of illusion was that? What kind of magic? Was the purpose of my life only to have birthed two children?' Whether she was babbling or speaking or merely talking to herself, Shivani did not know.

Dr Shergill kept listening. How was one to respond to such monologues?

'No. The purpose of life was also to raise those two children well. Silly girl! Who's taught you to say these ridiculous things? Even at thirty-five years of age, have you no sense?' The doctor's voice began to sound tender.

'Who knows. I've been this way since childhood. I probably won't change in my old age.'

'Ladies and gentlemen, she's started to grow old at thirty-five! Do you know my age? Two times thirty minus three. I am fifty-seven. Through all these years, I've felt myself change every day. Even so, do we change at all? What you call a magical world, I call the magic of the world. Look around you, it's the magic of the world at play everywhere! Reality is magical. The children I bring into this world each day, that's a kind of magic too!'

'Indeed, that's the most beautiful kind of magic. I understand that, but why won't I have a change of heart? Why am I so disenchanted by this magic? So much disillusionment?' Shivani lay on the check-up table, but her eyes were on a spider caught in her own cobweb, a foot above the AC vent.

'Ask your heart, then! Come, let's turn back the wheel of time. If we were to go back ten or fifteen years, what would you change?' Dr Shergill donned her gloves and walked towards her.

'Nothing at all. I want everything as it is. When did I say I had any regrets regarding life?'

'Passion then, if not regrets. We manage to live under any circumstance, pass the time, get through the years…' Dr Shergill's hands were now feeling Shivani's stomach as Shivani's monologue continued. As soon as Dr Shergill's hands touched a tender point below the lower half of her stomach, Shivani stopped talking and took a deep, difficult breath.

'Days, months, years go on, but we have to make something of this torrent of time. With our own hands … nobody else can build or destroy our lives.' Now Shivani was silent, and Dr Shergill was speaking.

The moment Dr Shergill's hands touched and pressed down forcefully on the lower right side of Shivani's stomach, Shivani grabbed them with her own hands. 'There … that's where the pain is.'

Extricating herself from Shivani's grip, Dr Shergill continued her examination. This time she was not as merciless when pressing her stomach.

'What do you think, Shivani? Is it the moments you can't get through or life?' Placing a hand on her back to support her, Dr Shergill now made her sit up.

'Maybe.'

'Girl! You don't have any problems. You're not a patient. How easy it must be for you to live in slow-moving moments! How easily your days must pass! The moments between seeing your husband off to work and sending your kids to school, those between breakfast and lunch, between dusting and gardening, between watching a daily soap and the evening news … everything so measured! So easy! So bracing! I fear the speed of time. I'm scared of all my hair turning white someday.' Dr Shergill now took out a pen and paper from her drawer and wrote her a prescription.

'Oh? Do doctors feel scared too?' Shivani asked, squatting on the check-up table, continuing to observe the spider caught in her cobweb a foot above the AC vent.

'Why wouldn't they?' Dr Shergill was now looking at something on her phone.

'It's just that I thought doctors are very wise, very intelligent. They have knowledge of pain, and they understand the process of healing.'

'Doctors can't heal themselves. Just like they can't cure the sickness of patients like you.'

'So, you and I are in the same boat then? We'll die like this, in wait for a good samaritan?'

'No, we'll keep living one day at a time. Dreaming our magical dreams. Aliens won't arrive to rescue us. I'm a doctor, so I can say this with certainty.'

'Don't say that, Doctor. My heart sinks. You're my doctor. You brought my kids into the world. You've seen my body from every angle. Who knows me better than you? There must be some cure for what ails me.'

'There is. Whatever little life you have left, prepare to live it. Do something out of the box … something wild … something that guarantees that you have no regrets on your deathbed.'

'Should I run away? That's one regret I shan't ever have. Should I board a train without knowing its destination? One that crosses stations with signs I can't read. Where nobody knows me. Where nobody needs me…'

'Bad idea. Come up with something else. Your kids need you right now.'

'A fling. Let's have a fling. A one-night stand. Like my husband's one-night stands.'

'Even worse. Talk about cutting off your nose to spite your face. The satisfaction and stability you never found in familiar territory in all these years, the hell you'll get it in a brand-new land in one night. Think of something else.'

'I can't. I can't think of anything.' Shivani lay back down again on the check-up table.

'You're a creative person. Look for a creative solution.'

'What do you mean?'

'I mean, conjure up a fantasy for yourself. A world of illusion. Search for your alter ego, your nemesis. Make them into characters and create a world to which you don't belong, but it belongs to you. In that world, choose your conditions for love. Plant tomatoes and lemons in the pots, along with seasonal flowers. Invent new ways of beating your breast about your woes. Put up an exhibition of cushion covers made from your saris. Paint images of your enemies onto your bedsheets. There are so many ways! Mix new colours into your tears, girl.'

'Here I am talking of leaving behind the world of fantasy and entering the real world, and there you are pushing me back into another dark, unknown well.'

'It's in the darkness that you'll see the light. From where you and I are sitting, everything is blurry. Neither radiance nor blackness, neither morning nor evening, neither darkness nor light. Have the courage to step into the darkness, Shivani. That's how you find the path towards light.'

'What was this? What sort of conversation did we just have? What kind of doctor and patient are we?'

'The kind that live their lives exactly how all the other women of the world do.'

'Really? Is that how all of them live? Doctors? And patients? In that case, I too will survive.'

'You and me and maybe that woman too whose twins I have to deliver in fifteen minutes.' Saying so, lady doctor Shergill donned her white robe, hung her stethoscope around her neck and exited her chamber, smiling. She came back just to say that Shivani, keep taking your medicines and before you come in for next month's appointment, get the invites for your exhibition printed.

Adjusting the pleats of her sari, Shivani thought that the only treatment for an incurable disease like life was probably life itself. A life that looked bland should be infused with artificial colours.

Then picking up the broom next to the dustbin in the corner, Shivani climbed up on Dr Shergill's desk and freed the spider swinging from the roof.

The Roommate

AMIDST THE INTENSE DISCUSSION IN THE CONFERENCE room, Aseema's phone rang loud enough to startle everyone.

'Why isn't your phone on silent? Mind your manners at least during a meeting, Aseema!' Akbar snapped at Aseema in front of everyone. But Aseema's complete attention was on the caller.

As soon as they got into the car, Akbar enquired, 'You look distracted. Is it because I told you off in front of the others?'

'No, Akbar, I need to make a call first.'

At the other end, Lily's chirpy voice was heard, 'For whom are man and wife so busy building a Taj Mahal in Dubai that they've no time to visit Mumbai?'

'We'll get one built for you if you like. But find yourself a Shahjahan first, to fund it!'

'I've found him. The wedding's in Patna in two months. Whether you're coming or not, we'll discuss later. But first, I have an important bit of news. National Geographic's airing my documentary tonight. It'll be broadcast forty minutes later in Dubai. Wherever you are, get home quickly, switch on the TV and settle in. More later.'

'Akbar, how long will it take to get home?'

'What's up? Are you feeling all right?'

'Lily's film is about to air. I don't want to miss a minute.'

The two of them reached home exactly five minutes before the film was to air. Settling little Aliza onto her lap, Aseema sat down before the TV. But she didn't pay attention to the film after all. Aliza had gone off to sleep in her lap and age-old memories had started stirring inside Aseema.

Putting Aliza to bed on the sofa, Aseema pulled her laptop forward. In its drive D was a folder that hadn't been opened in years. For some inexplicable reason, Aseema felt an urgent need to do so now.

The folder contained photographs from nine years ago. And all those poems and concept notes that Lily would spend her nights typing up on her laptop. The cache of memories that Aseema had preserved when she'd moved to Dubai was all in this folder.

Her first encounter with Lily had been odd.

'I'm Aseema, Aseema Contractor. The name sounds Hindu, but I'm a Muslim. I pray five times a day and fast during Ramzan. Does anyone have a problem with me living here?'

That was how Aseema had introduced herself. In the Four Bungalows area of Andheri, Mumbai, was a villa with a room for four women to stay in as paying guests. Three women were already living there. She had arrived to be the fourth roommate.

For two minutes after Aseema's question, there was silence, everyone on their own beds, lost in their own thoughts. The girl sitting on the middle bed broke the silence.

'I'm Nafiza D'Souza, Na-fee-za, not Nafiza. Being a D'Souza, I'm obviously Christian. The Miss sitting on the bed by the window is named Lily Pandey. Now how Lily is a Pandey, you'd best ask her directly. Sitting on the bed by the door is Vishakha Patel. She's come to Mumbai from Nairobi to learn Bharatnatyam. We don't know her caste or religion. She's found speaking on the phone sometimes in Gujarati and at other times in Malayalam. Her boyfriend is German. None of us have a problem with each other's names, surnames, castes or faiths. Now tell us about yourself, Miss Aseema.'

At Nafiza's sharp response, Aseema stood quietly for a bit. Then rolling her suitcase she entered the room and addressed Vishakha, 'Which one shall be my bed?'

With a glance, Vishakha gestured towards the bed next to Nafiza's. Aseema quietly started unpacking her things from her suitcase one at a time and stowing them in the adjacent almirah.

All the while, Vishakha stayed on her phone call, Lily worked on the newspaper's sudoku puzzle and Nafiza replugged her CD player's earphones into her ears. Nobody was in a rush.

Rush hour was in full swing the following morning at seven. Vishakha was running late for her class, Lily had to get to her shoot and Nafiza to her office. Nobody was willing to be up ten minutes earlier but everyone was down to argue for ten minutes about the bathroom. Aseema alone was sitting in her corner, ready to take on the day's grind. Holding up the paper as she read the previous day's stale news.

'Where's your office? Do you work or will you begin your search for a job today?' Nafiza lobbed the first question.

'No, I have a job. I'm an architect with Karmakar Architects. My office is in Worli. I'll leave in a bit.'

'So you're an architect. Even your name is Aseema Contractor. Is Hafeez Contractor a relative of yours?' Looking into the mirror, twisting her hair into a knot, hairpin clamped in her mouth, Lily asked Aseema's reflection with great earnestness.

For the first time since yesterday, a small smile was visible on Aseema's face in the mirror.

'I wish! I wouldn't have had to hustle this hard to get here,' she answered with a grin.

No sooner had Aseema said this than the mood in the room suddenly became lighter. It looked like it'd be possible for the four of them to cohabit. By revealing a vulnerable side to herself, Aseema had extended a hand of friendship.

'Come on, come and get breakfast, you all. It's milk and cornflakes today. Aseema, you'll be able to eat, right?' Kavita didi, the landlady, entered the room to summon everyone.

'I'm fasting during Ramzan, so I'll eat at night.'

'Yes, yes, you'd mentioned yesterday. Girls, Aseema will fast for Ramzan and read namaz. None of you have a problem with this, right?'

'Didi, if we don't have a problem with your daily cacophonous bhajans, why would we have one with someone reading namaz?' Vishakha replied. 'Now come on guys, else if I get late today, guruji will have me returned to this address like an unstamped envelope.'

One by one, they all left the house. Vishakha towards Malad to learn some more Bharatanatyam *mudra*s, Lily towards Aarey Colony to handle production for Creative Arts Films' daily soap and Nafiza to sit at JK Trading's reception.

In the evening, the aroma of kebabs wafted from the room, pakoris were being fried in Didi's kitchen and Aseema sat on her bed, cutting fruit in a plate on an old newspaper.

'It's time for *iftar*, Nafiza. I've got these kebabs. Would you like some? Didi's so nice! She's frying *pakoris* for me,' she said.

'Didi's nice because you're a spring chicken. Bit by bit, she'll extract the price of the cornflour, onions and salt being put into those *pakoris*,' Nafiza whispered.

'Really? Good thing you warned me. When do Lily and Vishakha get home?'

'Lily's usually late. It's often midnight by the time she gets back. She manages production for a primetime show on Star. When you have some time, listen to her dish out gossip about TV stars. And this Vishakha, her ex-boyfriend was a model. Have you seen that Nestlé ad? That hazel-eyed hunk? I'm forgetting his name. Veer Sappal, I think. He was Vishakha's boyfriend. He'd park his Enticer downstairs every day. I don't know what happened, they broke up. Now it's some German. But I haven't seen him.'

'I just asked when they'd get back, Nafiza.' Looking down, Aseema kept slicing and placing apples on the plate. On a finger on her left hand, a jewel gleamed.

'Are you engaged?' Chatty Nafiza neither got Aseema's sarcasm, nor could she stop her mouth from soliciting more material for gossip.

'No, I'm married. My husband's based in Dubai.'

'How interesting! So that's how you wear designer clothes. I did wonder – how much does this architect earn to have a whole wardrobe full of expensive clothes. Your husband's gifts, aren't they?'

Aseema raised her eyes and levelled a stare at Nafiza, but said nothing. However, she had understood that opening up too much to someone was equivalent to issuing an invitation for them to peep and peer into her life. This nosiness wasn't acceptable to Aseema.

No opportunity for conversation with Lily presented itself the entire week, and Vishakha didn't initiate one with Aseema. Noticing Aseema's silence and attitude, Nafiza too stayed within the limits of her territory in the room, on her bed.

The very next Sunday, Nafiza's resolve broke. Early in the morning, Lily asked her three roommates, '*A Beautiful Mind* is playing at Fame Adlabs. Russell Crowe is guaranteed an Oscar for it. Tickets for the morning show can be managed for thirty bucks. Who wants to join me?'

'I'm game!' Vishakha was the first to respond.

'Can I come?' Barely had she asked the question when Aseema was internally regretting it.

Once again, she was on her way to befriending her roommates, inviting them to peep and peer into her life. But the matter concerned Russell Crowe. So despite her many misgivings regarding friendships with roommates, Aseema went to Fame Adlabs with the three women.

After the movie, the outing continued with a long discussion over coffee and lunch. From the plot to the performances, from the screenplay to even the camera angles, Lily had something to say about it all.

'Looks like you're a prodigy too, Lily, like John Nash. I had no idea about your genius,' said Aseema.

'You ain't seen nothing yet, darling. We're still in the first days of our friendship. Will you accompany me to Juhu Beach in the evening? I'll display some more of my talents.'

On the brink of declining, Aseema assented. She was partly driven by a desire to pass time on a Sunday evening and partly by curiosity about Lily's spiritedness.

'You're not going to pull a Charles Herman on me, are you Lily?' Aseema asked laughingly, referencing John Nash's roommate who kept appearing and disappearing.

There was something about the girl that drew Aseema to her effortlessly. After spending the day roaming around Four Bungalows, in the evening the four roommates headed to Juhu Chowpatty on foot.

Lily kept up her chatter the whole way. The house in Patna, the hostel in Delhi, the village in Arrah, the set in Mumbai. Lily gave the other girls a tour of her colourful life.

Nafiza too narrated her story to them, how her mother had raised three fatherless daughters in a dilapidated one-bedroom house in Bhayandar. How, because of his drinking, her brother-in-law had abandoned her sister within merely four days of their wedding. How Nafiza had to become the sole earner for all her family of women.

'My life isn't rainbows and sunshine, girls. I've had to grind and hustle to make a life.' Nafiza said little but the eloquent Vishakha responded, 'Life's not easy for anyone. To live, you need a sense of humour, which you don't have, Nafiza.' These were the only words that left Vishakha's precious mouth that evening.

Even at nine in the night, none of the four had wanted to return to the PG. Though everyone shared bits of their lives, they were all captivated by Lily's stories. The people she encountered everyday, each one quite the character! Production manager Satish bhai had tried his luck in Telugu movies but was unsuccessful. Now he found unparalleled pleasure in organizing meals for Mumbai's artists and technicians. He spoke seven languages and kept forgetting which one to use with whom, speaking in English to the spot boy, in Gujarati with the director and in Telugu with Lily. The other party had to remind him which language to speak to them in. The serial Lily was working on was scripted based on whichever artist was available on set. If the artist was absent, the character would vanish from the episode.

As much as Lily talked, she also sang. Without rhyme or reason.

That night too, she regaled them – with a folk song that her mother would sing while rolling rotis. Sprawled on the sand, talking about her mother, Lily had started singing in her tinkling Bhojpuri, a song alluding to in-laws' taunts. On the sand, supported by Lily's voice, the other girls bobbed through their silences, thoughts and lives. There was only the din of the Chowpatty and the careless conversation between the sea's waves. Silence offers its own comfort, but careless conversation is the cement and mortar that binds relationships being built brick by brick.

A relationship was under construction between the roommates, but only two of them.

Now Lily turned to the new roommate, 'Tell us about yourself, Aseema.'

'My life isn't as flavourful,' Aseema said, but her voice carried neither Nafiza's bitterness nor Vishakha's helplessness. In this voice, there was a practical tone that could not be negated.

'I get malls made, buildings made. All the thinking about concrete has turned my thoughts to stone,' was all Aseema said.

'The stone shall melt in our company, Aseema.' Lily laughed, brushing the sand off her clothes as she got to her feet.

'The weekend's over. Tomorrow we'll see who goes off to break stones where, and who has the energy to melt stone. Are we leaving or is the plan to spend the night by the sea?' The bitterness in Nafiza's voice would return intermittently.

The week indeed weighed heavy on the roommates. Nobody was at leisure to meet or talk to anybody else. Nobody had time for anyone else. They were roommates, not friends. Vishakha would often stay over at her boyfriend's flat. Dealing with Nafiza's cynicism was difficult, so Aseema kept her distance. Lily was the only one to whom it was possible for Aseema to talk. But Lily's job was such that she'd return from shoots late at night, after everyone had gone to bed, and wake up in the afternoon once everyone had left for work. Aseema didn't think it was appropriate to wake Lily early in the morning. Yet she wanted to talk to Lily, to tell her to sing a folk song for her again. Aseema hadn't even asked Lily for her mobile number. Had she asked Nafiza for it, she would've goggled at her like Gabbar the beloved villain from the hit film *Sholay*, '*Bahot yaarana lagta hai.*'

When Aseema asked the landlady for Lily's number, she was direct, 'Why do you need it? Tell me, I'll pass along your message. By the way, it's best if you stay away from these three, Aseema. You're educated, respectable, older. Why bother with them?'

Aseema understood that the landlady didn't want the four of them to become friends. A friendship among them would mean a united front against her, a conspiracy. And if all four mutinied against her half-cooked dal and stale rice piled in the pressure cooker, then where would she be? That's why she'd been implementing the policy of 'divide and rule' among roommates for as many years as she'd been hosting paying guests.

One day, on rising for the *fajr* namaz, Aseema found Lily sitting outside in the drawing room.

'Are you up for namaz? Will you eat sehri? Drink milk? Shall I get them?' Lily asked Aseema as soon as she saw her.

'Sit, Lily. I'll manage everything. When did you get back?'

'Just a while ago. I'm unable to forget Nash's words, "Find a truly original idea. It's the only way I will ever matter." I'll have to discover an original idea, that's my only salvation. I can't do this TV serial stuff.'

'An original idea at four in the morning? It's Saturday tomorrow and Sunday the day after. Your show won't be on air. Think about this from tomorrow until Sunday. Now go to sleep. And give me your number before you do.' Aseema practically pushed Lily out of the drawing room.

Later that day, Aseema SMSd Lily that she would take her to Bhindi Bazaar for dinner on Saturday. Bhindi Bazaar's vibrancy during iftar hours is worth seeing and Aseema had, for many days, been craving Shalimar Restaurant's tandoori.

Lily SMSd back a 'Yes' to dinner.

She came to Aseema's office and the two boarded a taxi from there to Mohammad Ali Road.

'This'll be my first time eating with a Muslim during iftar, Aseema. You'd better deliver on all my high expectations,' said Lily, settling down in the taxi.

Within a short while, the two were at Mohammad Ali Road. From this end of the road to Bhindi Bazaar were colourful shops, stalls serving food and drinks, heaps of sweetmeats – there was a reason this Mumbai street had been christened 'Khaau Gully'.

Aseema took Lily straight to Shalimar. Tandoori raan masala and Shalimar chicken-chilly. Aseema ordered for both of them. For a bit, Lily was discomfited by the smell wafting from inside but her greed for the food kept her seated. As she mulled over something, a slight smile spread across her face.

'You know, Aseema, Papa had a Muslim colleague, Shahid Uncle. Whenever he'd leave after visiting Papa, Dadi used to have the seat cover washed with Dettol. He was given a separate cup, separate utensils to use. If Ma finds out I'm sitting here with you eating halal meat, she'll slaughter me.'

'Really, in the twenty-first century? Anyway, tell me what that Original Idea is that's been bothering you.'

'The idea for which I came to Mumbai. You know, I've been a film nerd since I was a kid. I was eleven when we got a VCP. I remember every film on Doordarshan. I'd watch them all. And on the VCP too, new and old films. Kids want to grow up to be doctors and engineers, but I wanted to join the movies. I remember being at my maternal grandparents' home for the summer. My uncle had got the tractor's battery charged so we could all watch *Ramayan* together. I went on strike, demanding that we watch the evening film instead. That's when I decided that I'd make movies about small towns, their dreams, their joys, their insecurities with sincerity.'

'So then, what's stopping you?'

'It's not that easy. Until Delhi, nobody had an issue with me moving out. Patna's just a night away. Besides, half of Bihar lives in Delhi. But for Mumbai, I had to put my life at stake.'

'I don't understand, Lily.'

'Papa said I could only come to Mumbai if I got married. I managed to get out of marrying, but not out of an engagement. My fiancé is in Powai, an engineer at Larsen and Toubro.'

'And ... what's the problem? You're in Mumbai, gainfully employed. Anyway, the only thing required for a good idea is your brain. Good thing you can take it with you anywhere you go!'

'The trouble isn't coming up with an idea, it's executing it.'

'That'll happen too. By the way, won't you introduce me to your fiancé?'

'Whyever not?' Lily asked in a pronounced Bihari accent. During affectionate moments, Lily's inner Bihari would emerge in full force. 'He's in London for a project. Honestly, the only reason I'm able to hang out with you is because he isn't around.'

Aseema deliberately ignored the sudden note of sadness inflecting Lily's words.

'All right, all right. He deserves your time. You meet on weekends, right?'

'Yeah. Anyway, let's go to Marine Drive? I'll tell you my Original Idea.'

'Let's! I'd do anything to listen to the Original Idea.'

Sitting by the sea at Marine Drive, Lily, for the first time, shared the story on which she wanted to base her film. Aseema said that were she a financier, she'd invest in Lily's film without a second thought. But since she wasn't in fact a financier, for the time being she'd invest her faith in Lily instead.

That much investment was enough for Lily.

Aseema didn't go home for Eid. The reason she gave was that the very morning after Eid, she had a meeting in Bangalore. But on the day, she took Lily to Haji Ali. After laying a shroud on the saint's shrine, Aseema cried, dupatta-draped head bent in prostration. Despite wanting to, Lily didn't ask why. On exiting from the dargah, Lily expressed a wish to go to the Siddhivinayak Temple.

'The Ganpati here grants all your heart's desires. It's Eid, whatever you asked the pir, ask Siddhivinayak too. It'll be like a reinforcement.' Lily laughed.

'What I've asked for, shan't be granted. Not at the pir's mazaar and not at Siddhivinayak,' Aseema said softly.

Standing in the queue for darshan, Lily tried unsuccessfully to read Aseema's expression, then gently said, 'I don't know what's bothering you, but I'm here if you want to talk, Aseema.'

Nobody said anything after that. They returned home by the afternoon. Kavita didi had prepared a special lunch. After eating, Lily took out a thick diary from her cupboard.

She announced, 'Today, I shall share this treasure with you guys. The poetry recital starts in ten minutes. Everyone to their seats please.'

Soon, all four roommates sat cross-legged on the floor. Lily began with Ghalib,

'Today my reasons for despair
I venture to share, but let's see if I do.'

'Listen to one from me,' Aseema declared, prompting a whistle from Lily. Aseema started humming,

'Neither can I let my eyes well up, nor sing songs.
Either way, my heart won't find peace and quiet.
Forget songs, were even my instrument taken away,
What I want to sing, oh! I cannot render it.'

Lily answered, 'It's an original, listen. Don't touch this knot / If it comes undone / Where will you float to / Is there a harbour there / Or a sleeping sea / We do not know.'

What had begun as a poetry recital progressed towards film songs; Vishakha sang a hymn by Mirabai and Nafiza belted out Celine Dion's 'I am Your Lady'. Late in the evening, the four of them went to sit in the park opposite.

'What a day! It was so much fun. It's good you didn't go home, Aseema,' Vishakha said.

'Your husband didn't come down for Eid?' Nafiza's question pierced both Aseema and Lily like an arrow.

'He couldn't get leave from work,' Aseema answered, lowering her eyes. Her fingers kept fussing with the lawn grass.

Lily gave Aseema a long, contemplative look, but said nothing.

That night, neither of them could sleep, but with the other two roommates present, there was no opportunity for a conversation.

The next morning, Aseema left the house. There was a message in Lily's phone inbox: 'off to Bandra, not Bangalore. family court. i'll be granted a divorce today. didn't know how to tell you. i'll go home to inform ammi-abbu in the evening. will talk when i get back in two days.'

With a heavy heart, Lily continued to get ready. On leaving the house, she hailed an auto to take her not to the Chandivali studio, but to Bandra–Kurla Complex. She waited outside the Bandra court for a long time, wrestling with a dilemma. Outside the family court of Mumbai, many families were on the brink of shattering and scattering. Lily had never seen a divorce take place, neither within her family, nor in her social circle.

What kind of adamancy must it take to break apart a relationship? What kind of jolt dislodged the rivets on which a relationship hinged? She had no understanding of how after sharing dreams under one roof, in one house, people could become strangers.

But Lily was worried about Aseema. She wasn't picking up her phone. Lily crossed the threshold and entered the court.

She didn't need to look hard to find Aseema. Her lawyer was with her, and standing some distance apart was her husband. Aseema was not at all shocked to see Lily. 'This is Adil, my husband. Though he won't be after the next hour.'

Adil carelessly extended his hand towards Lily. Feeling awkward, she quickly shook it and shuffled Aseema into a corner.

'What's all this, Aseema? I feel really cheated.'

'Even more than me?' Confronted by the tears swimming in Aseema's eyes, Lily couldn't say anything.

'Now that you've come all the way here, do me one more favour. Go home and pack for two days. Come with me to Pune. I need support to face my Ammi and Abbu.'

Lily was with Aseema on the evening bus to Pune. How and why were not questions Lily wanted to deal with right then.

Aseema started divulging everything to Lily in the bus.

Aseema and Adil had been together since college. They'd qualified as architects together. They'd got jobs at the same time. One day, Adil went to Pune and asked for

Aseema's hand in marriage. That's when they both decided to move to Mumbai. Adil opened his own firm and sporadically taught architecture. Aseema joined Karmakar Architects. They worked hard during the week and spent the weekends at Lonavala, Karjat and Mahabaleshwar.

But within a year, Adil started feeling the strain of marriage. The restrictions and accountability chafed at him. His family lived in Lucknow, making it difficult to solicit their support in strengthening the relationship.

'Architects are like performers, Lily. Just as their art can't be constrained, so their nature is unpredictable, totally free-spirited. At first, I used to cry and wail, fight all the time. My parents were going to come down from Pune to see us. Adil thought it appropriate to stay overnight at Madh Island with a female client of his. For the next two years, we kept dealing with ups and downs like that. At times, very close, other times, far apart. But then it all became too much to handle. Every little thing became an excuse for conflict.

'One night I returned from a meeting in Bangalore to find my suitcase outside the flat. The flat was locked from inside. I kept ringing the bell for an hour, but Adil didn't open the door. I roamed the streets all night, dragging my suitcase like a vagabond. Couldn't tell friends, couldn't call my folks. The next morning, I went to work, booked a guest house and began to hunt for a PG. All this while,

Adil ignored my calls and SMSs. I still kept going back every day, in the hope that he'd realize the error of his ways. Maybe we'd find a way out of this. One night, he SMSd me the word "divorce" thrice. Then he emailed me, and then sent a notice through the court to my office address. I still hadn't told anyone at home and went off to Italy for a six-month training. I got back and Adil still wanted the divorce. As you can see, today is the final chapter of my love story.'

But Aseema was unable to say all this in front of everyone in Pune.

Lily tried to help her explain. At times her family would listen, at other times they'd berate her. She would feel sorry for herself for getting involved, then wonder what she'd have done in Aseema's shoes.

Braving the storm, they returned together. Aseema hadn't wanted to stay at home for long.

Their lives were once again spent in anticipation of the weekend. But many a night, Lily would overhear Aseema sobbing, awake in the guise of doing namaz. She'd watch her try to find solace in the Quran.

But nobody else in the room had an inkling of what Aseema was going through. The four of them watched films at Fame Adlabs, met for lunch and dinner, even went sightseeing around Mumbai.

Once Lily's fiancé returned to Mumbai, these outings decreased. In March Lily had to go home for her wedding.

Aseema too had decided to move to Dubai and started applying for jobs. Even so, Lily would SMS her some couplet or other, signing off with 'just doing my roommate duty'.

'It has to be Dubai if I'm an architect,' Aseema stated one day, arguing her case for Dubai and showing images and 3D projections of the construction at Burj Khalifa and Palm Jumairah, widely considered marvels in the world of contemporary architecture.

That night, as was her habit, Lily went to Aseema to get an oil massage. Vishakha and Nafiza weren't back yet.

As she worked the oil into Lily's hair, Aseema asked about preparations for the wedding. Lily answered in monosyllables.

Disentangled from her hair, Aseema's fingers started massaging Lily's shoulders. Lily's eyelids involuntarily began drooping. Under Lily's thin nightie, Aseema's fingers started stroking the blue bruises surfacing on her neck, ones she'd been hiding under her collared shirt since yesterday.

Once her fingers had completed their probe, Aseema asked Lily, 'The fiancé whom you couldn't introduce to your roommate, whom you concoct a million reasons to not meet, after meeting whom you spend two days sick in bed – are these bruises the signs of that fiancé's love?'

Lily hurriedly scrambled to her feet. 'No, it's not like that. Shekhar just has a quick temper, that's all.'

That's all she could say. Shekhar was right, Lily didn't even know how to lie properly.

'And the consequence of that temper is that you walk around covering up marks? How do you put up with this, Lily? How do you live two lives?'

'I don't let the bruises on my body transfer onto my soul, that's how.'

'But for how long? I'm no relationship expert. If anything, I should have no right at all to dispense advice on relationships. But don't walk into fire with open eyes, Lily.'

Lily stayed silent. Then softly spoke, 'With two months left for the wedding, I can't do anything. I don't have the strength.'

'And yet you're strong enough to endure the destruction of your dreams, to quietly tolerate being beaten? Strong enough to throw into the sea the scripts you spend all night writing? Strong enough to accept the crumbling of your dream of making movies, that you've had since you were ten?'

The next day Lily phoned Patna, to announce her decision to call off the wedding.

The following week was a very stressful one. Lily grew exhausted explaining herself to Ma and Papa and then sundry uncles over the phone. An enraged Shekhar had stooped straight to maligning her character. All the TV parties where she'd introduced him as her fiancé, all the confidences she'd shared with the intent of being transparent, were all weaponized against her.

The way Shekhar behaved in the wake of their break-up made Lily sigh in relief. At least Shekhar's true face was out for all to see!

One evening Aseema SMSd Lily, 'The paradise we seek is out there!'

Then one day, Aseema left for Dubai and Lily left Mumbai for a few years to make Delhi her home again. Aseema got buildings erected in Dubai, while Lily was busy making documentaries in Delhi.

They kept in touch, but only as much as international calls would allow. After meeting and marrying Akbar, Aseema became occupied with building her business and with the arrival of Aliza, her world became condensed into the concerns of home and office. But certain relationships retain within us the warmth of the spark with which they'd first blazed, through distance and throughout lifetimes.

Over the past three hours, looking at the photographs, Aseema had relived those seven months that changed the course of her life. To her companion of those seven months, her beloved roommate, she sent many emails one after the other – with the old photos and script. And over the phone, a message with a smiley, '*Ghalib, it's the end of our despair* ... once again, just doing my roommate duty.'

Our Eyes Will Meet in Love

WHAT IS THE MOST DIFFICULT QUESTION IN THE world?

'How are you?'

How was one to answer such a dry and pointless question? If it was your mother asking you this, the question's difficulty level increased. If your mother asked this question on the seventeenth, twenty-seventh, sixty-seventh and one hundred and twenty-seventh morning of your married life with the same dedication, it was a disaster! How should an eighteen-weeks-married, ten-weeks-pregnant woman even answer? That too, to a mother sitting in a distant city in a faraway country, who had no inkling that Singapore was foreign in name only, and the same as Patna to live in. A neat and clean, orderly Patna glittering with high-rises. Her days, just like her mother's, revolved around four teatimes, three rounds of cooking, twice daily phone calls with her own folks and in-laws and one elaborate cleaning routine. Her clothing had changed, so to speak. There were other conveniences. She was free to be alone, liberated from the trapeze artistry involved in walking the tangled tightropes of a joint family.

Still, there were times when she missed Ma intensely. All her silent prayers to never lead Ma's life often came crashing down before her. Like today, when she must cook for guests in exactly the same way as Ma: a saucepan of Champaran mutton, a casserole of sattu parathas, a pot of moong dal halwa.

In such circumstances, how was she to answer to 'How are you?' The question fell like raindrops on her brittle heart and she sought shelter in the words, 'I'm fine, Ma,' to keep from slipping and falling.

Marriage is a knotty riddle and arranged marriage its illusory solution. Solidifying this 'arranged' process takes so long because by the time you reach the threshold of desire and passion, worldly concerns have taken over. Whether or not love blooms, compromise generally takes root.

Akanksha hadn't fallen in love and her marriage was too new to arrive at the threshold of compromise. It wasn't even that she was particularly young and naïve. Nor was it that her family had forced her to wed. Indeed, she had been given a good education, raised to get a proper job and prepare for a long-term career before the matter of marriage was brought up.

Akanksha had attended Patna's best school. The convent school was only three lanes, a crossroad and three neighbourhoods away from her home. She had attended the best college too, but that too was a women's college in her own city – another convent in truth. To her maternal family mushrooming around Patna, the possibility of the only granddaughter going away was unacceptable. That's why she had ended up doing her MBA from a private institute in Patna and started working in a bank in the city.

Her maternal grandmother, a patient of the lung and the heart, lived to see Akanksha get married. Had Chunnu Mama not somehow got her dementia-afflicted mind to see that these days good boys sought 'working women', even this minor freedom of being financially self-sufficient would have eluded her.

Thus, twenty-six years of Akanksha's life were spent within the twelve-kilometre radius of Kadamkuan, Ashok Rajpath, Kumharar Park and Kankadbagh. Every week, the women's special supplement of the local newspaper featured stories and photos of girls breaking barriers, and every week, some new barrier would be erected before her. This week, take a half day for a housewarming ceremony at Bitti Mausi's. On Tuesday, we have to propitiate the Hanumanji at the station, so don't be late. Either there was a wedding at someone's house, or someone was falling ill. The rigmarole of maintaining family relations was never-ending. On top of that was the eternal command against nightfall. It was only when she started working that she was able to have her curfew extended to half past seven. The concern about her getting into autos and rickshaws alone yielded some independence by way of a Scooty.

But these were all token forms of freedom. Akanksha's greatest fear was remaining stuck as a frog in the Kadamkuan well. Others might view marriage as a form of bondage, but Akanksha considered it the only path to liberation. She had seen how marriage had enabled her aunts and grandmothers to leave the cursed rut and suffocating boredom of their village and come to metropolitan bylanes about which they spread fake news on Facebook. This too was a kind of upward mobility!

More fortunately, to find a match, Akanksha's family finally drew up her birth chart, resulting in the discovery of her inauspicious birth. This news spread through their community at such speed that forget Patna – respectable families of Arrah, Chapra, Navada, Nalanda, Gaya, Jahanabad became impossible to reach out to. Ma's pride in her family in Delhi and Bihar evaporated in an instant. Finding a suitable boy for an inauspicious girl and expecting order in Patna's traffic are two ordeals difficult to overcome.

In this scenario, receiving a proposal from Aunt Soni's brother-in-law's brother-in-law's son who worked in Singapore, put Papa over the moon. Such a marvellous proposal for an inauspicious daughter! What was more, the boy's first wife had passed away in an accident, which meant that the stars portending ill fortune had been appeased. It's true that there was a nine-year difference in their ages. That was when Ma's guidance came in handy. After all, wasn't she eight years younger than Papa!

Even so, Akanksha tried her best to do background research. What the world conceals, the internet reveals.

Googling the strange name of 'Dinkar Pratyaksh', she scoured all his profiles: LinkedIn, Facebook, Twitter. Apart from his IIT-IIM profile pictures and weighty wisdom conveyed in Thesaurus-heavy English, she didn't find anything worth stalking. Not even photos from the first marriage.

It wasn't as though once the match had been fixed, there was any prohibition on the two of them talking. Before the wedding, they spoke plenty over WhatsApp and FaceTime. But like all freedoms, the curbs on this one too were predetermined. She was able to gather only enough information about Dinkar as was sufficient to say 'yes' to the proposal.

For Papa, just the fact of the boy being settled abroad was cause to celebrate, even if it was just Singapore. Akanksha wanted to tell Papa that it took more time to get from Leh to Chennai than it took to get from Kolkata to Singapore. But with the fixing of the marriage, as the entire family got busy getting their passports made, Akanksha began to understand the value of Papa's excitement about his Singapore-based, widowed son-in-law.

And then the wedding happened, in Patna. It was followed by the usual – first the reception, then the wedding night, then lunches, dinners and parties for relatives and friends.

Amidst this programme, time passed in such a blur that Akansha caught on to neither Dinkar's cryptic silences at night nor his insincere laughter during the day. The whole day passed in company and the night which she awaited with a beating heart came and went empty. She had outgrown the stage of harbouring callow curiosities about the mysteries of the flesh. But she wasn't of such an advanced age that she didn't seek companionship from the one she'd taken steps around the fire with. It might be Dinkar's second marriage, but it was her first.

But, true to his name, Dinkar appeared only during the day – bantering with his family, joking with his friends, sitting through long gossip sessions with his cousins – no secretive withdrawals, no awkwardness. When it was just the two of them, he was distant, as though carrying a big burden on his shoulders.

As night fell in their bedroom, his eyes would either attach themselves to the pages of a book or turn away and shut to the world. Akanksha understood neither her new bridegroom's silence nor its subtext.

One day she blurted this out while joking with the cousins. No sooner had the paternal cousin-in-law made a quip about the blossoming colour of the pink she wore that Akanksha remarked, 'If only your brother would notice his second wife.' A silence deeper than the one produced by Dinkar descended on the faces of everyone in the room.

That night without any preamble, Dinkar turned himself towards Akanksha. Too soon, he loosened his embrace. She wasn't sure if this was an invitation or the revenge of his bruised male ego. All she was sure of was that whatever happened was extremely mechanical. She was also sure that there must be some fault within her that she had failed to attract Dinkar.

Then one night, she finally asked him, 'Do you not like me?'

Dinkar gave a curt response, 'In an arranged marriage, it takes time.'

For the next few days, their programme continued – of banal but deceptively normal conversations by day and abnormal, robotic sexual relations by night. Whose were those lucky fingers that leaped to touch each other? Which were those colourful butterflies responsible for fluttering in one's stomach in the throes of first love? She got neither the restlessness nor the butterflies. She got only a passport and the name inside it – Mrs Akanksha Pratyaksh.

They arrived at Singapore together. Dinkar went back to work and Akanksha got busy trying to convert his fancy condo from a bachelor pad into a family home. On the first day, she tried her best to find traces of the first wife. But nothing. There wasn't a single piece of memory or nook of grief in the house. It was probably for the best. Crying over one memory made it difficult to see the future. In barely a few weeks of marriage, loneliness had sedimented in the gap between them, with much left unsaid. But the blade of separation was too blunt to slice through the darkness of their silences.

After wrapping up the day's chores and emailing job applications, there was nothing to do. So once Dinkar left for work, Akansha took the bus to Mustafa Market and spent more than half the day finding excuses to look for Patna in the Little India neighbourhood. Today she needed jasmine incense sticks, tomorrow it was orange pekoe tea. The next day, it was yellow mustard seeds she needed to cook fish, and the day after that an iron saucepan. There were a thousand reasons to roam around in Mustafa and not one to return home.

And anyway, Dinkar would leave early and get home late at night. She had heard that in Singapore people worked eight-hour jobs as though doing a favour to companies. What sort of bank was Dinkar's that gave him neither time in the morning nor reprieve in the evening? Even once home, he looked hassled and harried. All discourse between the two of them was distant and desolate. If by chance her laughter landed in the void, it sounded raw and scratchy. She sometimes felt that Dinkar was punishing himself for some sin, especially on occasions when their tentative rapport was on the verge of turning into a friendship but never quite did.

Like the evening Akanskha fell sick in Singapore for the first time. The weather there was strange in March. As the northeast monsoon was on its way out, rain was followed by increased humidity. The hot-and-cold seasons of Magh-Falgun and Ashwin-Kartik that Ma would caution her about in Patna lasted all year here. And so, here she was, running a fever.

In those two days, Akanksha became certain that Dinkar wasn't a bad sort. He was merely in the habit of walking about with meaningless sorrows in his moist eyes. There's a word for people like this in English – masochists. Those people who take pleasure from inflicting pain on themselves.

Apart from this, Akanksha was convinced that there was something wrong with her. She didn't love Dinkar enough to follow Asha Parekh in serenading Rajesh Khanna, 'Take my sorrows, I'll take yours / I'll live a little, so will you.' Directing all her energies towards chores, she tried to make up for what she lacked.

Devoting herself to domesticity was part of this mitigation. Cooking delicious food, changing flowers in vases every other day, tidying Dinkar's wardrobe and other messes – this became her goal. And part of an ineffective campaign to woo Dinkar.

She wondered how favourably Dinkar viewed these attempts. In any case, there was enough comfort between them now that on the weekends his friends flocked to their home. Indian men consider an arranged bride's toils in the kitchen their birth right, expected to satisfy their gourmet palates and bottomless stomachs every weekend.

On top of that, they only played music of their own choosing. It was not just their mentality that belonged in the hoary past. Even their musical tastes were from the Dark Ages! Dinkar read books predating Ramdhari Singh 'Dinkar' and listened to ghazals. The first time Akansha heard a lady croon 'I saw my lover everywhere' in a raspy, masculine voice on Dinkar's speaker, she had to quietly Google the Farsi and Arabic lyrics in the middle of making rotis.

That day, while loading the dishwasher, she mulled over how popular people who listened to intellectual songs and read poetry ended up being so heartless and desolate in real life. How could one who sought the beloved in the almighty be blind to the angst of the living, breathing life partner perennially at his service? The Patna boys who rolled up their car windows and blasted Badshah's tracks onto the streets seemed a better deal. At least they were exactly who they appeared to be. No façade. No artifice.

But then, she never really had the chance to find out how exactly Patna boys were. Had she loved, had she rebelled for love, she'd have known how different boys in love were from who they became in wedlock.

Akanksha too had become something else. Cohabiting with Dinkar more as a flatmate than a wife, she cultivated hobbies similar to his. Hobbies like discovering and listening to old ghazals and songs. As far as refined musical interests went, her upbringing in Patna had familiarized her with just a handful of voices: Mohammad Rafi, Mukesh, Kishore Kumar and Lata Mangeshkar – at the most Jagjit Singh and Pankaj Udhas. She had grown up on a diet of Bollywood. She watched movies either on Set Max or Zee Cinema or at Krishna-Regent-Elphinstone with family or friends. Dinkar had opened up a new world to her. Binging on Korean dramas on Netflix and hunting down and listening to old ghazals on YouTube – this had become Akanksha's new Singaporean routine. A new way of biding time.

And so, she settled into a rhythm until one day, a couple of months into her expat life in Singapore, it struck her that while she PMSd like clockwork on exactly the twenty-fifth day since her last period, she hadn't got her periods on the twenty-eighth day this time. She hadn't felt the need to use protection of any kind, but nor had she wanted to plan a family this soon. The thought of conceiving hadn't even occurred to her during the ten-fifteen minutes of mechanical sex. She had imagined that baby-making was something that people built up to with lots of affection, after a great deal of lovemaking.

Obviously, like most of her half-baked notions of life, this too turned out to be false. The line on the home pregnancy kit was not one of confirmation but on the horizon of a yawning chasm of confusion. She didn't even know whom to turn to. What would she even tell her mother! And what about Dinkar? By accident … by circumstance … perhaps by mistake … I'm carrying your child?

The first thing she Googled was: Is abortion legal in Singapore? Turned out that it was legal for citizens of Singapore. Or for those holding an Employment of Foreign Manpower Act work pass. Or for those who'd resided in the country for at least four months. And for those whose lives were endangered by the pregnancy. She didn't belong to any of these categories. Her life was indeed in danger, but how could she prove this medically? By jumping from this twenty-first floor condo?

She had no option but to tell Dinkar. Late at night, after clearing the utensils and putting away the leftovers in the kitchen before heading to bed, she somehow gathered the courage to say, 'I am pregnant.'

She received an eight-word response – 'This is why I didn't want to marry.' So saying, Dinkar upped and left for the study on the pretext of work. Akanksha was left in a corner of the bed – broken, scattered, abandoned.

The next morning, everything was the same, it was as though nothing had happened. This is the problem with pregnancy. The responsibility lies with two people, but only one of them bears it. Still, Dinkar did make an appointment with a gynaecologist before going to office, and returned early so he could accompany her to it.

In the car, Akanksha asked him, 'What do you want to do?'

Dinkar explained the whole plan to her. The delivery should take place in India. Being born in Singapore didn't grant citizenship, so what was the point? Had it been the US or Europe, it would have been a different matter. Once Akanksha had spoken to the doctor, she could decide whether she wanted to leave for India right away or closer to the date of delivery: 'I am okay with anything.'

I am okay with anything? It was so easy for Dinkar to say this!

'But I am not okay. I am not okay with anything.' Akanksha's anger exploded like grains from a broken glass jar. Shards. Grains. Neither could be picked out.

Akanksha wouldn't meet the doctor that evening. Dinkar turned the car back towards home. And told her that she should decide what was to be done. Whether she wanted a child or didn't, she would have to go to India either way. She had the right to choose.

The right to choose? What sort of solution was this? And what was she going to tell her folks in Patna? That the sex in her marriage was loveless, that was why she didn't want a child? Or that after two months, she couldn't figure out the man she'd married? She couldn't even say that she didn't want to come back. Keep me or throw me out of the house, but being alone is better than suffocating in a lifeless marriage. At least she would breathe!

But she couldn't muster the courage to tell anyone this. She still had a week to decide. And to pretend to be happily married during that week, because a distant cousin of Dinkar's was coming from New Jersey to Singapore for work and would be staying with them.

Dinkar had been preparing for the visit for many days. The guest room's curtains were changed. The bar was stocked with wine. The fridge was provisioned with varieties of frozen meat and fish. On the fridge was tacked a menu to ensure that the guest was served something exquisite for each meal.

With the arrival of Dinkar Pratyaksh's cousin Himanshu Shekhar, the atmosphere at home changed completely. Dinkar's days were once again full of relaxation and fun. As for the nights, he had a solid excuse for staying away. Citing Akanksha's pregnancy as the reason, Dinkar would sleep in the other room. He didn't even bother to put up a show for his cousin.

Akanksha couldn't understand why she awoke in the middle of the night. She normally kept a bottle of water by her bedside, but that night she felt more thirsty than usual.

She had read on the internet that dry lips and excessive thirst were among the symptoms in the first trimester. It was this thirst that pushed her in the direction of the kitchen.

She should not have gone. She should not have even got up. She should not have passed the guestroom on her way through the gallery. Had she not made the mistake of getting up that night, she would have been saved from coming face to face with the most painful moment of her life.

Somehow, the door of the guest room had been left ajar. Dinkar and Shekhar were sleeping together on the queen size bed inside. Not just lying asleep together, but intimately entwined. On spying the easy and sensual way in which Dinkar's arm was wrapped around Shekhar, Akanksha stumbled. In that one microsecond, she felt as though she'd stop breathing and her heart would leap out of her body. In that one microsecond, she felt her feet freezing into ice and darkness looming before her eyes.

Getting to the kitchen from the guestroom, she suppressed her hiccups with great difficulty. As soon as she splashed the chilled water from the refrigerated bottle across her face, hot tears began to flow. Rage, humiliation, sorrow, fear – all mixed with her hiccups and tears.

That night, Akanksha understood one more thing. There was nothing lacking in her. Whatever was lacking – if it could even be called a lack – was in Dinkar. The realization that Dinkar could not love a woman felt like a blow to her guts. That night, she had another epiphany – Dinkar's first wife was not the victim of an accident. She could not accept this tragic twist in her life, and had chosen death.

On the heels of this sudden revelation, Akanksha's anger and frustration once again found release through her tears. Who had given Dinkar the right to play with so many lives? What level of carelessness was this that he was going to drag another potential life into this game borne of his cowardice?

This was the question that Akanksha served Dinkar with his tea and without preamble the next morning, right in front of Himanshu. They were both stunned. Dinkar's tongue became stuck to his palate, as though Akanksha had added glue to his tea.

Dinkar remained silent, it was Himanshu who spoke.

As teenagers, they had both realized that they were different from other boys. At the age when boys secretly smuggled naked pictures of women into bathrooms, Himanshu and Dinkar searched for their existence in the works of Walt Whitman and Alan Ginsberg. In the large courtyards, snug rooms and close-hewn walls of Ghazipur, the truth could not remain hidden, that there was something between them that should not be. Not only were they both boys, but they were related. Not one sin, but two. They hadn't come out even as adults, so it was no surprise that as boys of fifteen and sixteen, they didn't have the ability to declare that what lay between them was pure, natural, unblemished. And so, ducking and diving, they would meet during the holidays and explore each other's bodies in a meaningless attempt to find themselves.

The first time, their middle uncle caught them together. Locked in a room, they were beaten so badly that it took months for the wounds to heal. But a far deeper wound had been inflicted on their hearts. Dinkar was forcibly sent to Delhi for IIT preparation and Himanshu's father moved heaven and earth, sold his entire property to send him far away to America.

The family was relieved that the matter had been resolved. Both sides of the clan decided never to bring the topic up with each other or any outsider. This was that family secret which, with great effort and endeavour, had been buried deep in the layers of time.

But that which is pure, doesn't lose its shine despite being subjected to every challenge. This was the case with Dinkar and Himanshu. Dinkar burnt the midnight oil to prepare for IIT exams because this was the only way he could imagine being able to reunite with Himanshu. He had quietly resolved that on the other side of his four-year IIT programme, his next destination would be the US.

But his mother threatened to drink poison. He could settle in any part of the world, but she would not let him go to the US. It was with great difficulty that they agreed to let him move to Singapore. And this too, probably because they thought there would no overlap between Dinkar's investment banking job and Himanshu's biotechnology career. Or perhaps with the thought that despite being a developed nation, Singapore wasn't modern enough to have legalized same-sex unions and gay marriage. Despite this, Himanshu and Dinkar kept meeting. In different parts of the world, in different cities, in different beds. What never changed was their partnership, their love for each other.

On hearing all this, Akanksha felt an intense envy. Why had she never loved anyone with this passion? Why had nobody ever wanted her in this all-consuming way? What sort of love was this that could never be exhibited and expressed by those who felt it? Or perhaps that was why their love persevered. That which is forbidden is all the more precious.

And then Akanksha asked what she should not have, 'Did she die or did she take her life?'

'That's one thing I'll never forgive myself for,' was all Dinkar said before he started crying. He wept his eyes out, to the point of illness. Himanshu wrapped his arms around Dinkar to comfort him and, with hitched breaths, kept kissing his forehead and tears.

Akanksha was completely outside the radius of Dinkar's thoughts, guilt, regret or indeed any emotion. Forget love or friendship, they hadn't even forged a bond based on human feeling, that she could go over and take him into her arms. Before the hurt and humiliated girl inside her could screech her accusations at her again, Akanksha got up and went into her room.

After replaying the events of the past few hours in her mind, she understood the real reason for her sorrow. She realized that more than hurt, it was envy that was burning her up. Her envy was directed at that bed, at that room, in fact at the sense of peace that they together embodied, which Akanksha had never known. It was the sort of peace that could be experienced by witnessing two people in love. The peace that she would see in her father's expression when he did little things for her mother.

The image of Dinkar with his peacefully asleep face buried in Himanshu's neck swam before her eyes. She had never seen such innocent softness on Dinkar's face. Himanshu's kisses on Dinkar's forehead stabbed her in the chest.

Having cried out all her anger and hurt, it occurred to Akanksha that this was not her defeat. This was Dinkar's cowardice, his defeat. Akanksha would take her revenge, but on her terms. She bathed, slathered cream all over her body, wore her favourite clothes and lipstick and finally emerged. Then in a calm and stable voice, she addressed Dinkar, 'Invite your friends over this evening. You two are together. You must celebrate. As it is, the three of us are experts at keeping up appearances.'

All dressed up, Akanksha went into the kitchen. Whatever Dinkar and Himanshu discussed behind her back, she had neither care nor curiosity for. Her focus was on making Champaran mutton and sattu parathas. Though the onions for the mutton weren't ready today, fragments of the dark clouds swirling about in her mind were sieved. Preparing sattu for the parathas, tears exceeded the caraway and pickle in the masala. That was why when her mother asked, 'How are you?' over the phone, she answered with the automatic, 'I am fine.'

She was not fine. But she had to become fine.

As dinnertime neared, the house began to echo with laughter. Akanksha had by now exhibited all the talents of an experienced host. Following music, alcohol, homemade kebabs and an accounting of sale and purchase of companies around the world, the dinner was a hit too, as was the dessert of moong dal halwa.

As midnight drew close, the guests began to leave. And then there were three – Dinkar, Himanshu and Akanksha. After setting the living room to rights, she poured out a glass of wine each for Dinkar and Himanshu, dimmed the lights and set Begum Akhtar to play on the speaker – *Come to my chamber, beloved / Our eyes will meet in love.*

And then leaving them there, she left, closing the door behind her.

Begum Akhtar kept pace with her footsteps swiftly walking down Clark Quay beside the Singapore River. Shimmering buildings fell and sank into the river. On her fingers she kept count of the weeks and months that she had yet to plan to get rid of. On her phone, she searched for the cheapest flight to Patna. And on her airpods, Begum Akhtar crooned softly,

Your memory came to me like a tear
In these desolate eyes
In the wilderness of good fortune
It does still rain
Come to my chamber, beloved
Our eyes will meet in love.

The Blue Scarf

SHAMBHAVI QUIETLY WENT ABOUT GETTING HER things together. On the bed was a jumbo-sized suitcase and a scatter of colourful, ironed clothes waiting to be organized. Three months wasn't a lot to pack for, but every moment of foreign travel demanded that one be prepared – according to weather and custom.

In any case, Shambhavi had an obsessive-compulsive desire to do everything by the rules. Her clothes were neatly folded, mindfully worn and carefully stored. Whatever was concrete and visible had an inbuilt order – like the containers, fruit, vegetables and utensils stacked in the fridge … the kitchen drawers … the living-room cushions … the flowers in the vase … the life she and Amitesh had built over the years.

The abstract was unruly – relationships, the heart, happiness, sorrow, regret…

Amidst the order of the clothes, what abstract dissatisfaction was the blue silk scarf fluttering on the floor protesting against? Her glance falling on the scarf, Shambhavi unthinkingly balled it up and stuffed it into her handbag.

That dratted scarf … a cruel reminder of so much! Memory was one heartless butcher. Untimely and irrational, it had this bad habit of slicing and chopping: the heart, moments and experiences. How tenacious were memories that they defied our attempts to capture them, slipping away here and there, and yet adhesively clinging to our identities. Impossible to wash or wipe.

This time, the blue scarf had become entangled with a tree of memories from the branch of which dangled a date. 26 December.

Shambhavi shivered at the memory of the sweaty softness of her fist entwined with Amitesh's fingers. The blue scarf reminded her of that Wednesday seven years ago, when holding Amitesh in one hand and an empty glass of cold coffee in the other, she had sucked bubbles up through the straw as they roamed around in Janpath. There was no special reason, but Shambhavi remembers that that Wednesday, 26 December fell on the fifth day of the first month of her marriage.

Shambhavi had yet another obsessive-compulsive tendency – of remembering dates. Things, facts, faces, events – she knotted all of them up with dates and stowed them in her mind. That was why she couldn't forget dates. That was why she vividly remembered that she'd bought this blue silk scarf on the twenty-sixth of December in the course of romping about Janpath.

This blue scarf was just an unnecessary accessory. Why had she bought it?

Why had she got married? And why had this thought suddenly popped up in her mind? Then again, random thoughts were often devoid of logic.

Shrugging off the memory, disentangling it from the blue scarf, Shambhavi returned to packing, when a red jacket lying at the foot of the bed triggered another memory … a fight she'd had with Amitesh on 12 January of the new year.

It was a senseless fight. Over a jacket. It was too small. It was too big. The material was inferior. It was too expensive. This long-drawn-out argument went on for thirty five minutes, after which Shambhavi bought the jacket at Amitesh's insistence, to keep the peace. It was another matter that she'd worn it only thrice. Red made her nauseous.

Why was she recalling all this today? She didn't want to take these memories with her on the plane, which was why Shambhavi draped the red jacket on the hanger and hung it in the closet.

During this time, she had managed to recall that the day this jacket had been bought was also the day the two of them had ordered curtains for the house. Sky blue curtains with a golden shimmer. 'Like the golden rays of the sun sweeping across a calm sky,' Amitesh had said after they'd put them up. The drawing room still had them, though Shambhavi now hung white bamboo curtains in her room and Amitesh's room had blinds.

Not only the curtains, but their relationship had changed as well. Though turmoil scarred the interiors of their home, its facade appeared intact and well-maintained. Sunshine peered through the clouds like clockwork. But the sky had been divided. Living quarters had been separated. Each basked in the sunshine in different time zones. So much so that often despite being in the same room, they weren't in the same place.

'When are you back?' Amitesh had asked from the bean bag after a long period of sitting silently, watching her pack. Questions were useful when there was nothing to say.

Amitesh sat in the room in the hope that Shambhavi would express something while preparing to leave – a longing, a regret. A command, a directive. But when silence became a habit, ignoring the other person came easy.

'You know when,' Shambhavi answered curtly. Without raising her head, without looking Amitesh in the face, into his eyes. When there was nothing to say, it was difficult to come up with adequate responses to questions.

Amitesh fell silent and leaned his head against the wall, sitting on the bean bag and attending to the sounds made by Shambhavi's packing. But, after all, how much sound did clothes make as they were folded and arranged in a suitcase? He gave up and returned to his room. His room, which he still referred to as the TV room. Despite having stayed in that room by himself for months, sleeping and living there.

When two people shared a house, though they may occupy it alone, they made a habit of each other's presence. The company of another was our biggest need, even if it was an illusion. Living with illusions and going to bed each night under the covers of romantic fictions was the greatest truth about life. Certainly about marriage, if not life. The fear of separation and the yearning for the return, someday, of the separated – that's what marriages were built on.

Shambhavi was leaving for three months, just three months … this wasn't a separation, Amitesh told himself. So why did it feel like she wouldn't return? It might even be better for them to separate rather than have her leave one day and return the next like this. Amitesh's contemplations saddened him. Even if one were to launch search-and-rescue missions for relationships in danger, what was to be done about the painful memories they carried?

In her room, Shambhavi was struck by a sudden wave of melancholia. Fading mehendi, the dusking day, sunlight descending from the mountains, a poem nearing completion, a coffee cup about to be emptied, holidays speeding towards their end, a train pulling into its destination, the last bit of effort to get over a tiny crush, and a beloved preparing for a long journey … even one of these images was enough to cause the heart to sink!

Shambhavi stuck a list onto the fridge. Housekeeper, cook, carpenter, clothes presser, plumber, security guard, hospital, corner-shop, even numbers of restaurants for home delivery. In all these years, Amitesh had never realized how much work it took to run a house. He'd discovered the housekeeper's name a month ago and that too because Shambavi had left a note on the table, 'Please tell Kanta to come at three today.' A curt, extremely formal note. Like Shambavi's handwriting. Like Shambhavi's distant but polite and calm attitude which Amitesh had got used to living with.

Running the washing machine, giving clothes to the presser for ironing, taking out the garbage, serving food in the two blue pottery plates, getting the curtains cleaned for Holi and Diwali – he couldn't recall when Shambhavi had started being this way. Formal. Curt. Distant. Silent. And though Amitesh didn't want to admit it to himself: indifferent. Utterly apathetic. To the point of callousness.

But the house was running … without Amitesh knowing how much the presser charged for ironing. What the housekeeper's wages were and whom to call to order 10 kilos of flour. For the next three months, Amitesh would have to manage all that.

Who knew what he'd have to do in three months! What if in these three months he was to get used to living without Shambhavi forever? What if Shambhavi didn't come back?

The car screeched to a halt outside the airport. The silence filling up the house that had been bundled into the car was now rent by the sound of the brakes. Followed by the noise of car doors being opened and the suitcase being dragged from the boot, there was sudden commotion.

Shambhavi may not have been dwelling on it, but Amitesh's inner conflict was writ large on his face through the car ride. On the way to the airport, he had thrice taken a wrong turn. If he had his way, he'd have turned the car back home. But then, when had he ever had his way, especially with Shambhavi!

Taking the suitcase out of the boot, Shambhavi quickly dragged it towards the trolley. There was no rush. There was still time for departure. But placing her luggage onto the trolley, she proceeded towards the entry gate without a word to Amitesh. He didn't try to stop her either. He kept gazing after Shambhavi's retreating form until the deep velvet of the blue scarf around her neck disappeared into the crowd of colours. Amitesh's heart now felt as empty as his house.

Inside, there was a long queue at check-in. As it was, there were a million hassles at international airports. Customs cleared and luggage checked in, Shambhavi took her boarding pass and settled down in a corner with her laptop.

There was still time for departure. Enough to accomplish many a task. Emails could be answered, friends could be chatted with over GTalk, then there was random yet necessary work like commenting on people's Facebook status messages, and using witty tweets to pick up threads with friends in the virtual world.

But having never done any of this for years, why would Shambhavi resume any of it now, in the next two hours? She didn't realize when being reserved outside of home had become second nature to her. She fell into that routine, half-heartedly reading office emails and replying to them disinterestedly. Surfing here and there. Then for some reason, she clicked on a folder titled 'Photos'.

Perhaps it is in transit that we are closest to our memories. Or we want to be. Nostalgia in its purest form hits home when one is travelling away from it.

Linked to this trip, memories of many of Shambhavi's previous life journeys were stored in this folder. Of before her marriage, of the wedding, the honeymoon, friends, family and those events that she kept archiving in her memory year after year.

Seven years of marriage, seven years worth of dates, and that one date that changed everything as though it were destined. This brokenness, this devastation … and living with that devastation through a sense of incompleteness, a loss which Amitesh was now feeling keenly.

The thirteenth of February. Shambhavi remembered the date all too well. She remembered because she'd missed her period due on the third of February. After some days of waiting, she had come to her senses and had her fears confirmed by a self-testing pregnancy kit. Fears that had kept Amitesh awake all night.

'We can't. It's too soon Shambhu,' Amitesh had anxiously said, perambulating up and down the room. 'We have so much to do. You have a career. I am building mine. We're not ready. We just can't.' Amitesh had kept talking and Shambhavi had kept listening. Frozen. Her brain wasn't working. Yet she had made a habitual attempt at pushing back.

'Why aren't we ready? You're thirty-four, I'm twenty-seven. We're the right age, isn't it?' Shambhavi had enquired but her voice had held a forlorn note of defeat.

'We've been married for less than three months. I'm not ready and that's that,' declaring an end to the argument, Amitesh had thought it appropriate to exit the room.

After that, the two of them had stopped speaking. As though this was all Shambhavi's doing, as though she alone was responsible and had to make a decision.

Amitesh had left for two weeks, leaving Shambhavi alone with her dilemma. She had been unable to decide whether to rejoice or weep at her condition, to prepare for the arrival of her child or to pray for it to bid her farewell. How those two weeks had passed…

Shambhavi had given her mother-in-law the good news over the phone, thinking that perhaps she would be able to persuade Amitesh. She had announced the news of her four-week pregnancy on every possible forum. Perhaps if everyone knew, Amitesh would have to accept it. She had been foolish. Decisions weren't made by airing them before all and sundry, but calmly, in private.

In any case, no tactic worked once Amitesh came back. He had been adamant. The people who'd been congratulating her, advising her to take care, over the past fortnight – all those people had changed their tune when Amitesh returned.

Ma had tried to make Shambhavi understand over the phone, 'If you weren't planning, you should've been more careful. You have to spend your life with him. What'll you do with a kid he doesn't want? I can only comfort you.'

But she didn't need comforting. Even her mother-in-law, ecstatic at her pregnancy and praying for blessings, had stopped talking to her. Whom else could Shambhavi turn to! Whom could she confide in about the cracks in a three-month-old marriage! Who would even listen to her!

For two check-ups and an ultrasound, she had gone to the clinic alone. Who knew what the sonologist had made of the tears streaming out of the corners of her eyes as she lay on the ultrasound table! When she had got up, the sonologist had finally asked her, 'You're married, right?'

'I wish I weren't!' Shambhavi had exclaimed as she left the room.

Amitesh had taken Shambhavi to the doctor one time, but only to get information about an abortion. Dr Sachdev was a friend's aunt so it was safe, he had said. Dr Sachdev had tried her best to counsel them against the idea. But during the check-up, Shambhavi's liquid eyes had disclosed everything. Amitesh had taken the appointment for an abortion for the next morning.

That night, Shambhavi's eyes had rebelled. Not a single teardrop had emerged even as her heart wept buckets. Why was she so powerless? Her own husband had deemed this child an orphan and now slept soundly right next to her. A marriage was a million experiences rolled into one!

Shambhavi had remained calm the next morning too. Amitesh had made small talk in the car. Plans for new furniture and wall paint. Updates on his new project. Maybe this was his way of maintaining normalcy. It was possible that Amitesh was just as troubled and this chit-chat was an ineffective method of hiding his inexpressible sorrow. But even sorrow ought to be shared. When we ceased sharing our sorrows, we withheld ourselves from each other.

And so Shambhavi had listened to Amitesh's monologue. In any case, these were his plans alone, not shared ones. What they had shared, was to be lost today. A shared night. A shared love. A shared life. Shared sorrow.

At seven in the morning, Shambhavi had met the doctor for an abortion.

'You're seven weeks pregnant, Shambhavi.'

'I know. I know that the baby's heart is probably being formed right now, its brain too. I know its eyelashes have probably begun to develop, and folds in both elbows.' Shambhavi who hadn't said a word all the way here, had now unloaded before the doctor.

In a moment of stillness, Dr Sachdev had regarded Shambhavi with a steady gaze. 'There's still time for you to reconsider,' she had said contemplatively.

Shambhavi had remained quiet, closing her eyes as she leaned her head against the wall behind the chair.

Dr Sachdeva had called the nurse and directed her to complete the procedures preceding an MTP. Once she had changed, Shambhavi was laid on a stretcher and taken to the operation theatre. Placing her palm on her stomach for the last time, she had asked her unborn child for forgiveness. Bidding it farewell, she had stated that she was prepared to accept any punishment meted out to her. Closing her eyes for the last time, she had shoved her tears back. By this time, the general anaesthesia had begun to work and Shambhavi had fallen into an abyss.

When she had come to after the abortion, she was in the recovery room. Amitesh was holding two packets. One had sanitary pads and the other juice and biscuits. Despite wanting to, Shambhavi hadn't been able to turn her face away.

The events that followed seemed to be on fast forward mode. She had no memory of how many days she felt weakness and how many days the bleeding lasted. All she remembered was that in that state, Amitesh had sent her home to her mother's.

'Who'll look after you in this condition? The house is too small. We can't ask anyone to move in. I'll be travelling, how will you stay by yourself? This is exactly why I said it wasn't the right time for a kid.'

Shambhavi had answered everyone's questions alone. She had endured the pain alone. She had tried to tend to her anguish by herself. The pain might have lessened with time if she had shared it with Amitesh. But he had left Shambhavi alone with her guilt, her despair. Maybe that was why she hadn't been able to forgive him. But she couldn't forgive herself either, for not taking her own decision. It was easy to forgive others. Forgiving yourself and those you considered your own was the hardest.

And then somehow, daily fights had become the norm. The act of sharing a bed with the one she had pledged to spend her life with had taken on a ceremonial form.

And life had gone on. To deal with the irreducible pain, Shambhavi had drowned herself in work. There was no way out of the marriage, nor any impetus for her to make a decision. She had let time flow past.

Oblivious to the cracks in his relationship, Amitesh had scaled the ladder of success one rung after another. 'Time heals all wounds' – faith in this most useless of philosophies could keep one going, but expectation without faith could be devastating.

But Amitesh had faith that everything would be all right in the end. That was why, believing everything to be normal, he too had thrown himself into work. He hadn't expected to accomplish so much with his business in such a short period of time. Within three years, each of his efforts and ventures into e-commerce had been successful. The loan had been paid off, life improved. Or at least that was what his bank balance and the increasing size of his car had indicated.

One day, Amitesh had arrogantly said to Shambhavi something which, instead of closing the gap between them, had widened it to an extent that would be difficult to overcome.

'We can plan for a kid now, Shambhavi. In fact, I would say quit your job and start focusing on the coming baby,' Amitesh had said, mixing the Thai curry made by the cook with brown rice.

Shambhavi had said nothing, and had retreated into the bedroom with her dinner plate.

When we aren't speaking much to each other, we tend to say the wrong thing at the wrong time. The salty liquid had streamed from Shambhavi's eyes into her brown rice.

She had kept eating quietly. The evening's promise was the mere hope that everything would be okay. A hope devoid of any faith.

The colour of hope had appeared as a line on the pregnancy test kit next month. But this time, for some reason, Shambhavi hadn't said anything to Amitesh, or anyone else. She had kept going to work as usual, for sixteen, sometimes eighteen hours a day. As if nothing had happened, indeed as though there was apprehension about something happening.

And then one night that which Shambhavi had dreaded since that time four years ago, when she had lain on the table in the operation theatre, had happened. She had started bleeding in her sleep. Amitesh had become agitated. The next morning when they both reached Dr Sachdeva's house, she had told them to head to the hospital immediately.

After consecutive ultrasounds, they had got to the root of the problem. The sonologist had called Amitesh into the examination room and showed him the condition of Shambhavi's womb.

'We didn't know about this pregnancy, Doctor,' Amitesh had said, almost embarrassed. The sonologist had looked at Amitesh long and hard, without saying anything.

After a blood test and some more check-ups in the next half hour, Shambhavi had been taken to the operation theatre. Both the infected embryo and her fallopian tube had been surgically removed.

Shambhavi was once again in the recovery room. Once again, Amitesh had stood before her holding juice and sanitary pads.

'I've spoken to the Doctor, Shambhu. There won't be any problems. You can conceive. Removing one tube doesn't change all that much. You're not worried, are you?'

This time, Shambhavi had turned her face away. The tears pouring down were of regret. She should have put up a fight the first time, dug in her heels, saved her child. She should have made her decision that first time.

Ever since that hospital visit, the distance between the two of them had kept increasing. Shambhavi wasn't ready to meet anyone, neither a gynecologist, nor a psychologist. Every time Amitesh suggested consulting a doctor, Shambhavi would say in a low voice, 'We need a couple's therapist or a lawyer, not a doctor.'

Amitesh now remained silent. Who knew who was at fault and how long the punishment would last! Amitesh too must have dreamt of a better life … but when two people were on opposite ends of a decision, there was no way to reconcile. They could only walk parallel to each other.

Time had flown as before. Both of them had built their own worlds in separate corners of the house. Only the EMI was shared between them.

Then one day Shambhavi had received an acceptance letter for a three-month fellowship and had prepared to go abroad. Rather than trying to bridge the gap that had turned into an abyss, it was better to go far away. Even if it was for a short while. Perhaps staying apart would help her think clearly, make decisions.

The ring of her cellphone snapped Shambhavi out of her reverie. It was almost time to board her flight. She picked up the call after it rang a few times.

'Have you checked in?'

'Hmm.'

'Are you leaving in anger?'

Shambhavi hung up without replying.

After this point, her phone internet would stop working in the other country, which was why she opened her email for the last time.

Seeing Amitesh's name in the inbox, she shuddered. Before they were married, she'd count the minutes between Amitesh's emails. Once he had gone on assignment to Bangalore. It wasn't possible to chat in the office, so they'd email each other. There would be an email every five minutes. Even during her meetings, Shambhavi's mind would be on her inbox. This fever pitch of their romance lasted from the eighth of March to the sixteenth of August. Shambhavi hadn't forgotten those dates either. On the sixteenth of August, while eating at their engagement party, Shambavi said laughingly to Amitesh, 'I said "yes" because of your emails. You're not half as interesting as them.'

Amitesh would always flirt by email. He had proposed over email too. They had planned the wedding over email. This time too, after all these years, to present his case and explain himself, Amitesh took the support of an email. For a long while Shambhavi stared at the screen. It crossed her mind to delete the email without reading it. After all, what difference would this explanation make?

Even so, she opened it. The email contained attachments. Shambhavi set them to downloading before beginning to read.

Shambhu,

I know you're very upset as you go. I also know why. Please don't think of this as an excuse, but I've attached some papers for you to look at. A bank statement and a copy of an agreement I signed yesterday.

After meeting you, I wanted to give you a good life, for which I had to take risks. That's why I quit my job to start my own company. I didn't want you to live in a rented house, so I took a loan and used all my savings to buy a house. I know that after we got married, I wasn't able to give you all those things we'd dreamed of together. But I was trying my level best, Shambhavi. I didn't want to share all this with you at the time, lest you worry. You were distressed anyway. You can hold me responsible for not having our child, but

I couldn't bring one into our unsettled life and increase our burden. Especially not yours.

We have no control over some things, not even our own feelings and responses. At times I was unreasonable and other times you were hurtful. But we still love each other. Else you wouldn't have left those numbers on the fridge for my convenience.

Finish your fellowship, travel the world. Till then, I'll set our house up for a child. Come back. Soon.

There were three attachments with the mail – a bank statement, a project agreement and a song. Before she could listen to it, she heard the announcement for her flight's departure.

Shambhavi closed her laptop. She could only think of this: if they had both protected their child and somehow fought for their family, their firstborn would be six years old today. Now Shambhavi didn't blame anyone but herself. Our destiny was ours, as were our decisions.

Shambhavi took her boarding pass and proceeded for boarding. The blue scarf left behind on the seat too made its peace with its destiny and with Shambhavi's decision.

About the Author

Anu Singh Choudhary, a celebrated author in Hindi, is also an accomplished screenwriter. Her experience as a documentary film-maker and award-winning journalist make her stories an authentic chronicle of the zeitgeist. Anu has written extensively across mediums: print, radio, TV, films and digital. As a screenwriter, Anu has co-written *Aarya* seasons 1 and 2. She has also co-written the critically acclaimed Disney+Hotstar series *Grahan*, inspired by a Hindi novel, *Chaurasee*. She has written the Hindi screenplay adaptation of the Malayalam masterpiece *The Great Indian Kitchen* and has adapted two Bengali films into Hindi. As the co-founder of Dopamine Media, Anu has written and directed *The Good Girl Show*, a five-part series for YouTube, and has co-produced *Alma Matters: Inside the IIT Dream*, a three-part docu-series streaming on Netflix. She is the author of the bestselling

Hindi books *Neela Scarf*, *Mamma Ki Diary* and *Bhali Ladkiyaan, Buri Ladkiyaan*. She has translated well-known authors such as Perumal Murugan, Namita Gokhale, Paulo Coelho, Vir Sanghvi and Anuja Chauhan into Hindi. Anu started her career in journalism with NDTV. She has been awarded the Ramnath Goenka Award for Excellence in Journalism and the Laadli Media and Advertising Awards for her stories in *Gaon Connection*.

About the Translator

Kamayani Sharma is an independent writer, researcher, translator and podcaster. She graduated in philosophy from the University of Pune and holds an MA from the School of Arts & Aesthetics, JNU. Her critical writing on visual art and cinema has appeared in publications worldwide, as well as in peer-reviewed journals and edited volumes. In 2020, she was a finalist for the International Award for Art Criticism and in 2022, she received the Kalpalata Fellowship in Visual Culture Writing from the Kamala and Ganesh Sitapati Trust. Her poetry has appeared in *Fulcrum: An Annual of Poetry and Aesthetics*, *Stinging Fly*, *Cha: An Asian Literary Journal*, *Pratilipi*, *The Kartika Review* and *14 International Younger Poets*. Sharma runs ARTalaap, South Asia's first independent visual culture podcast (Instagram: @art.alaap).

30 Years *of*

HarperCollins *Publishers* India

At HarperCollins, we believe in telling the best stories and finding the widest possible readership for our books in every format possible. We started publishing 30 years ago; a great deal has changed since then, but what has remained constant is the passion with which our authors write their books, the love with which readers receive them, and the sheer joy and excitement that we as publishers feel in being a part of the publishing process.

Over the years, we've had the pleasure of publishing some of the finest writing from the subcontinent and around the world, and some of the biggest bestsellers in India's publishing history. Our books and authors have won a phenomenal range of awards, and we ourselves have been named Publisher of the Year the greatest number of times. But nothing has meant more to us than the fact that millions of people have read the books we published, and somewhere, a book of ours might have made a difference.

As we step into our fourth decade, we go back to that one word – a word which has been a driving force for us all these years.

Read.

Harper Collins

HARPER PERENNIAL

HARPER BUSINESS

HARPER BLACK

हार्पर हिन्दी

HarperCollins *Children's Books*

HARPER DESIGN

HARPER VANTAGE

Harper Sport